THE BRIDGE

by Mary Faderan

ISBN:

978-1-0879-6718-9

CHAPTER ONE

Looking at Paris in this light reminds me of what I felt long ago as I stood in the growing dusk by the bridge in Paris, saying goodbye to my past self. The waters of the river Seine were rushing below me as I peered over the stone edge of the Pont Neuf. My tears fell into the large abyss of the waters that carried them away and made them insignificant. My feelings poured into all those tears

that represented a lifelong dream that
ended when Paul left me. I no longer
cared if I lived to see where the rest
of my life would end. I knew I
couldn't hurl myself into this rushing
water. I didn't want to go that way,
I thought. I stopped crying after a
little while and then I stood
straight. The sun dipped below the
horizon and soon the little white
lights would come out from the windows
of the buildings that stood beside the
river bank. I pulled my coat closer in
front of me and stepped away from the
side of the bridge. The tears on my
face were dry. I still felt this
gaping hole in my heart and I knew
that it would be a long time before I
would recover from the loss of Paul

Trent.

I walked slowly down the side of the bridge and took the lonely Metro home. The crowds of the day had waned and I was able to take solace with my thoughts in a huddle inside the shaking car on the way home. I tried not to contemplate what I was going to be coming home to. I lived alone in a third floor apartment in the Rue Maritain. It was a comfortable place that was handed down to me from a rich and wealthy Great Aunt named Solange Louvier. Solange Louvier was a Baroness in the noble classes. Her favour on me was a happy one. She liked me of all the children that she had in our large family. My parents, already passed on, were her favourite people and being the only child, she knew that I might have a lonely life when I grew up.

The tears came unbidden to my eyes but I averted my gaze and tried not to think of past lives. The therapist had given me that piece of advice. Dr. Prince told me that an hour ago. But I now just remembered it. Somehow his therapy session seemed to have escaped my memory. Now that I remember his kindly words I felt a bucking up of my mood.

There was a small restaurant on the way home and I went there to pick up some bread and cheese, and a large

container of home made soup that
Madame Cortes made for her customers.
Tonight's soup was garlic and onion
with some herbs and a few fragments of
chicken breast. It made my mouth
water at the thought of having this
for my evening meal. She was in the
back of the restautant but she waved
at me when I came in to browse.

I didn't wish to linger so I made
my purchase. Then I left and made the
short distance to my apartment house.
I made my way up to the third floor
and fumbled for the key. I fitted it
into the lock and turned the knob and
entered. The ambience of my apartment
was cold due to the lack heat. It
annoyed me slightly but it was a fact

of my life. The people who made the
building were ancient and the current
owners did not bother to upgrade the
heating so I had on the thick sweater
and leggings that I had on for the
day, and discarded my woolen coat on
the back of the door.

I looked for my cat, Sylvie, who
was a rather thin tortoishell who
resembled a Russian but she was too
little in size. I found her in a
shelter several years ago. She was
curled up by the fireplace inside the
knitted afghan that I liked to throw
over my knee as I sat and read my
novels of romance in the armchair.

Sylvie gave a wide yawn when she

saw me. I scooped her up and gave her a kiss before letting her go back to her afghan.

The phone rang and I answered it briefly. "Hallo?"

"It's Dorian, I'm calling to find out if you have any plans to visit the lab tonight?"

Dorian was one of the scientists who worked in the laboratory that employed me. I was a technician there.

"No," I answered, stifling a frown. "I am home for the night."

"Drat," she said with a sigh.

Then she went on to explain. A rather
convoluted story about how she was
unexpectedly entertaining her
boyfriend, Roalph, who was from out of
town. Her experiment was needing a
change in buffer and she needed
somebody to do it for her. "I guess
I'll call someone else. Are you sure
you're not intending to come back to
the lab?"

"I'm sure."

I hung up after she rang off and
said to myself, "What does she think
of anyone there, they're her lackeys?"

It made me mad to think of her,
so very beautiful and slim, with hazel

eyes and black hair cut short in the
mode of the season. It was their good
fortune to catch the men they set
their caps on and I was one of those
who watched feeling left out. It was
terrible that my love affair didn't
work, and now I had nobody to love. I
became depressed again. I sought out
the dinner I brought home with me.
The act of preparing the meal took me
out of my depression and then suddenly
out of the blue, the skies broke and
thunder and lightning came over the
city. Torrents of rain came down and
lashed the windows and the pavements
below. It was a good idea wasn't it?
Yes it was!

    After a good meal, I took my

antidepressant and changed into my
flannel pajamas and sought out another
romance novel from my meagre
collection of books by the side of my
bed. I started from where I stopped.
The story was about a woman who was a
foundling adopted by a rich nobleman
and his wife. The story was very
heartwarming and I became less aware
of my own troubles. By the time I got
to read the last sentence on the page,
I fell asleep.

It was a dreamless sleep. I awoke
the next morning feeling refreshed. I
felt as though I was carried away from
the sadness of my visit to the
doctor's office and taken out of my
depressed situation by the goodness

that I received in my little
apartment.

Sylvie jumped on the bed next to
me and started licking my hair. I
laughed at her and said, "No, Sylvie,
you cannot groom me today." But I
hugged her and she was purring in a
quiet way against me and swished her
long mink-like tail in quiet
affection.

It was time to get ready so I let
her go. I had a thought that today
was going to be the first day of the
rest of my life. With that, I got up
and energetically made my way to the
bathroom to start this new day of my
life.

Chapter Two

I was not the type of girl who
let herself go with this depression.
I had been depressed as diagnosed by
the doctors from the time Paul had
left me. It was about seven years ago
when I was nineteen. I suffered a
collapse and went to the hospital
where I stayed for five weeks. The
experience was unnerving. Never in my

life had I thought I would be in the same dwelling with inpatients suffering from a range of psychological problems like manic-depression, schizophrenia, suicidal tendencies and depression like mine. It was only my ability to be calm and enduring that I was able to get through it. I had a visit from my neighbor Colleen Draft once in a while. I went through the weekly visit with the doctor I was given, *Madamoiselle Le Docteur* Grammond, who was a nice enough person. Then I went through group therapy which was conducted by a woman whose name escapes me but she wore a stylish sweater set and skirt at all times. I had art therapy with a woman who wore

her hair long and dry, and was clad in
the sort of peasant style that was in
fashion decades ago. Then the big
doctor of the unit would conduct Grand
Ronde each Monday and gather all the
patients together. He never really
spoke to me except for one time when
everyone was finished and people were
flocking to the doors to leave the big
meeting room. He was Monsieur *Le
Docteur* Ramon Villez, and he saw me
and said suddenly, "Agnes, you know
what's wrong with you?"

I was taken aback. What did he
mean? I wondered. "What is wrong
with me, Doctor Villez?"

"You are a shy girl. That's
what's wrong with you." He
pronounced. He looked rather like a

cartoon character with a bristle mustache and large horn rimmed glasses. Then he swept out of the room and I stood silent apart.

This thought that I was shy was preposterous to me now, I reminded myself as I stepped out of the Metro and headed up the stair way to the main Avenue. Paris was teeming with activity at eight in the morning, I noticed. I barely got through the crowds that I met on the way to work. "Why would I be shy?" I demanded of myself aloud. "I think they have no classification of shyness in that stupid DSM book they have," I concluded with finality.

The laboratory was that of Doctor
Grantham, who was a transplanted
English scientist from Oxford. He
hired me after I left the hospital.
He was a good person, I thought. He
worked on the problem of Alzheimer's.
This was a popular topic of research.
Many of his people, the scientists,
were from different countries. I
worked as one of his staff who was
assigned from time to time to work
with one or two of the visiting
scientists. My main work was in the
immune system of mice that were
treated with a new drug to treat
Alzheimer's. It was part of the
overall work of Michel Crelon who was
famous already for his doctoral thesis
which he received from Spain's famous

University of Madrid.

The building of the laboratory,
called Laboratory Risen, was located
on Rue Fortnum. It was a towering
glass and steel edifice. I hurried to
the revolving doors and then passed
through the large reception and lobby
area, and into the waiting elevator
that would carry me and several other
people to the twenty-second floor.

The moment I stepped onto the
twenty second floor, I was met with a
warm gust of air, which oddly
comforted me. I went to one of the
laboratories in the hallway near the
stairwell and got inside. It was a
large room, with stations for four

scientists or technicians. A desk and some shelves, then there were benches as they called them which held either a machine or space upon which to do stuff on. There was already a person working there, Renee Belson, who was a timid-looking woman in her fifties. She was Crelon's main technician. Her work was impeccable. She wore her hair in a bun at the base of her neck, and her clothes were usually in the fashion of the day, but with a certain conservatism. She glanced up at me and saw that I was wearing a pair of leggings that were colourful and a black long mannish sweater. She tried not to frown at my outfit. It never failed to make me take a step slower when she would glare at me from over her half-moon spectacles. "What's wrong?" I asked.

"You." She said coolly, facing away from me and meddling with an instrument. "You and your silly outfits."

"No they're not silly. They keep me warm. I'm always cold here."

"Oh, well, I think you'll never get a man if you kept looking like that."

"I'm not sure I care for a man who wouldn't like my outfit." I replied with some heat. I wanted to stamp my foot but that was too

childish so I didn't. I headed for my
desk and put my bag away inside a
drawer. "I'm going to shop for
something so you'll like it. What do
you recommend?" I eyed her outfit
under the lab coat that she wore.
"What is that you're wearing today?"

    "I'm wearing an old outfit."

    "Yes it looks old."

    "Oh you are rude today. What
happened last night?"

    "Nothing."

    "Ok, today we are having some
guests. Michel has people from

Oxford. The big boss is out of town. I wanted to warn you to wear something nice."

"I won't speak to these people I don't think."

"No you won't. Now that you're dressed like that."

I gave her a moue' with my mouth. "I think you're a mood today. I will ignore you all day long. Go and have lunch with these visitors and I will have a peaceful day."

"Just try to look decent once in a while. They'll never promote you."

"For what?"

"I don't know. Michel tells me I can go with him when he sets up his own laboratory."

"I see. Well, I'm not interested in traveling to some place in Spain to live as a promoted individual."

"Ha. I love Spain."

"Fine."

"You might just meet a nice man from Oxford today." She smiled slightly.

"Oh really? No." I remembered

Paul and a pang of something welled up in my chest. "I think not."

"Oh ok. I'll be here for a while to set up this instrument and then I will be heading to find some pastries for the visitors. Michel said that they will be presenting some data at noon. You do want to stay for that, of course."

"I'll take good notes." I said with a smile. I decided not to take her rudeness so seriously. I thought she was nervous about the visitors. She was, after all, a divorcee, and was on the lookout for another husband. These women were always on the lookout for a husband, I thought

with some irony. I wondered at my
thought and then decided I was headed
for the proverbial shelf. The bus was
about to leave and I had not a ticket
to take the trip.

The door opened suddenly. The
man who opened the door was a tall and
rather hulking sort and his energetic
entrance had created a stir in that
the door had escaped his grasp and
swung against the wall behind it,
hitting the wall with a bang.

Dr. Michel Crelon, I said to
myself. He always had a big entrance.
He was over six feet tall and did not
know his own strength. There were
instances when he would carry out an

experiment on his own where he would damage something due to his ungainliness. But he was smart and everyone excused his bull-in-the-China shop mannerisms.

"Hello, ladies, how are you both?" He asked with a smile. His face was shadowed by a beard and his cheerful blue eyes peered through wire-rimmed glasses.

"*Bonjour*, Michel," Renee said as she glanced up at him.

"*Bonjour*, Renee. I've had news. Hello, Agnes," he greeted me. "I've had news. We're having a team from Oxford come by today. They'll mill around but mostly they'll hold a few presentations for the group. I want you both to attend as always. Now,"

He paused, warming his hands as he
rubbed them against each other.
"Agnes, you need to present yourself
at about four thirty this afternoon.
There will be someone who might want
to find a place to eat and you'll show
them the neighborhood, eh?"

I looked at him, hiding my
disappointment. I would have been
longing to get home at that point in
the day.

As if reading my mind, Michel
added, "You don't have to coddle them,
just take them somewhere then tell
them how to get back to the lab and -
or - how to get back to their hotel."
He didn't wait for me to answer. He
turned away and went to Renee's desk.
"I'm hoping you've got the order in

for lunch? I'm eager to get the presentations for the luncheon."

Renee said, "They are going to be there."

"Good."

He went back to the door. "I'm going to enjoy these visitors."

"How many guests are we having?" I asked hastily before he left.

"Oh, three."

"Ok."

"Do we have any more information who they are?"

Michel nodded. "Yes, I will ask Helene to send an email with their CVs. They're a great team. Happy about them coming to visit."

"How long will they stay?" I asked, half-curious. I wasn't sure

how to think of the new Oxford Team.
Part of me wondered whether they would
have any connection with Paul. But
that seemed far-fetched. Paul was an
artist.

"Oh, they'll be here all week.
I'll drive them to the airport Friday
after lunch and they'll be gone by the
end of the day." Michel looked at me
with a long look and then he turned
and left. Then a half-minute later,
he returned. "Where is Dorian?"

Renee and I looked at each other
and we both shrugged. "We don't
know," I replied.

Michel shrugged as well and left.

"Good, they'll be here and then
they'll be gone," Renee said with a
dismissive tone.

"Good, I agree." I went back to what I was doing in my desk. There was a list of things to do that had to be attended to. Why did I think of Paul again? I shook my head. I needed more distractions today, I decided.

I felt a rumble of hunger in my stomach and so I decided a nice croissant from the downstairs cafeteria would be a good thing to have before I started the day's work. It wasn't something I did regularly but it was a means to fortify myself for the day if the day were going to have too many people to spend time with.

I decided not to tell Renee where I was going, but then I thought Renee might be sad if I came back with food.

Renee was impossibly thin and this was her big achievement in her mature life. I asked, "I'm getting a croissant from the cafeteria. Do you wish for one too?"

"No, I'm fine. But get me a *cafe au lait*."

I made a small face. Coffee for two would be a challenge - how did she expect me to fetch us both a coffee and a croissant for myself? I asked myself crossly. But I went off and walked down the hallway to the elevator. I saw a few technicians from other labs and greeted them cheerfully.

"Hi, Agnes, how are you?" One of them asked. She was carrying a large jug of buffer.

"Oh fine." I waved at her and got into the elevator.

The cafeteria was a well appointed place, filled with lovely breads, several stations of coffee and tea, and a hot line of food that consisted of small pastries, some egg sandwiches, several kinds of souffle's. The chef, Bernard, was presiding over it all with his tall white hat and the handlebar moustache that hid half of his Latin face.

He ignored me for he wasn't interested in me - I wasn't interested in him - which seemed to bother him anyway. It was not my habit to commiserate with everyone. I held myself aloof from people as much as possible. It was another side effect

of my failed romance with Paul. Again
his name came to me and it was not a
pleasant thought.

The words of Dr Prince last night
came back to me. "Forget this man,
you've had enough time. Try to find
someone else. I'm sure you have still
all the charms of femininity. Go and
date people there are too many hours
in a day. Don't dwell on the past."

I tried to reason with him. "I
don't think I can ever forget Paul."

"Well, he forgot you by the time
he married that woman who he then ran
off with to live in England. Stop
trying to revise the past and think he
was somehow pretending to be involved
for some strange fictional reason."
Dr Prince said testily.

"Ok," I replied, slumping in my chair.

The croissant was huge and then I had to get two coffees. The woman who was at the end where the cash register was smiled at me briefly. "I'm in need of a carton to bring the coffees up. Can you tell me where I can find them?"

She gave me an irritated look. Then when I kept staring at her, she pointed to a table near the beginning of the line. "There they are."

"Thanks," I replied trying not to lose my temper at her reluctance to help. "What is she for but to help people?" I asked myself in an undertone.

I was happy to bring Renee her coffee. I figured it would put her in a good mood. I settled in my chair and stretched out my arms before getting to my laboratory notebook. I bit into the large croissant and inhaled and tasted the goodness. A French croissant in Paris, I said to myself. Mmm. I was lifted out of my sad thoughts and proceeded to go through my list of things to do for the day.

The door opened as I was making progress with my croissant. It was Dorian. I didn't have to turn around. Her perfume wafted into the room before she did. "Hello, girls,"

Dorian said in her sweet and high-
pitched voice. "How are you both?"

"Fine," Renee and I said in
unison, not looking up.

Dorian said nothing but I felt
waves of dislike from her. I wondered
if she was going to come to talk to me
and I braced myself. Dorian and I
didn't like each other very much.

She stood by my chair and I felt
as though she was willing me to look
at her. So I did. She stood silently
looking at me with a false smile on
her face. Dorian wore an elegant
sweater dress and her hair was, as
always, coiffed in a chic bob.
Finally, she spoke, "I had to come in
last night to check on my column."
Her work was a convoluted project and

if I cared I would have said something there but I let her speak. "I'm really disappointed that you weren't able to come to help me. Roalph was here only for a short time."

Roalph was her lover who lived somewhere out of town I cared less to find out about where.

"I took an early afternoon off," I replied, hating that I had to make an excuse. "I'm very sorry Dorian. You might have told me earlier and I would have made an effort to change my schedule."

She stared at me and then she flounced off to her desk where she intentionally made a commotion by throwing her things aside before she settled into her work.

Renee spoke and said, "You might have asked someone else, Dorian. I was here till eight o'clock in the evening. When did you call Agnes?"

"Never mind!"

Dorian hunched over her desk and put her spectacles on her face. Her silent figure was the one thing that made Renee and I feel out of our comfort zone in the laboratory. I silently prayed for Dorian to be taken away from our lives. She was so full of falseness I doubt she really had the results she showed to people during lab meetings.

Before too long, Dorian flounced out of the room and we never saw her until the time the guests from Oxford came in.

Halfway through the morning I
went to the women's lavatory to make
sure that my appearance wasn't too
shabby. I stared at myself in a
critical manner. I saw staring back
at me a woman of some youth who wore
her streaked hair that used to be
brown wearing a shapeless sweater. I
bought this sweater some years ago
from Bennetton. My eyes were hazel
and I had a straight nose. My mouth
was a bit too large for my face but it
was shapely. I had good skin which
sometimes tended to pallor. I
wondered whether I needed to put on
some lipstick but Renee would only
approve so I didn't. I was glad that
I had shoulder length hair which I've

been able to put up behind my head to keep the strands from falling over my face whenever I did an experiment. Satisfied with my appearance, I went out and surveyed the hallway.

Down a few yards away was Michel Crelon leading a group of men wearing what was distinctly English clothes. They were more conservative in appearance and wore neckties. They had someone with them who looked as though he were their leader. A man who was in his seventies, and two other men who looked much younger.

Michel saw me and gave me a signal to join them. "Ah, Agnes, you're just in time. Here's our Oxford Team."

The men looked at me curiously.

The old man smiled slightly and gave a
nod.

Michel went on to give
introductions. The old man was Dr
Felix Sydnor, the Head of their
Alzheimer's team. He in turn
introduced Ronan Michaels who looked
attractive when he smiled, which was
what he did when he shook my hand.
His hand seemed rather dry to the
touch and enclosed mine in a warm
squeeze. The other man, who seemed to
have a problem with his throat which
bobbled as he swallowed nervously. His
name was William Lisdon.

"Ronan here is our expert in
biochemistry and Trevor is our expert
in protein purification." Spoke Dr.
Sydnor.

Michel was quite excited from his manner. "Agnes is one of our top technicians. She might benefit from a small consult with one of you, if you have time."

"I'm sure we'll be happy to meet with her and anyone else in your team," said Dr. Sydnor pleasantly. "Could we possibly trouble you - we are in need of refreshment."

Michel led them away and I stood briefly to watch them disappear into one of the lavatories.

I was mildly interested in the team. I could learn a few things from them. I sighed and went back to my laboratory.

Renee was not anywhere in sight. But Dorian was back. Despite my

reticence to volunteer information, I
spoke, saying, "The Oxford guests have
arrived."

"Oh?" Dorian asked, and I felt
as though she was in a better mood.
"What were they like?"

"Oh, they are English."

"Oh. Well that's ok," she
shrugged. She was busy fiddling with
her column. "I'm thinking my column
has turned dry. I'm really upset
about it. You should have come when I
called you."

"Really, Dorian, why do we have
to hash out the past?"

"You're the technician, Miss, I'm
the one who needs to tell you what to
do," Dorian turned to me and put her
hand on her hip. This made me mad but

I kept my composure. "I can write you up with Michel. Just you wait."

"Oh really? Why don't you do it? I'm not afraid of you."

"You will be," her lips thinned into a smile.

"Go to hell," I muttered under my breath.

She asked, "What did you just say?"

"Nothing," I went to my desk and made some movements to pretend that I was searching for my notebook. But her manner unnerved me. I wasn't happy she would be so evil. She was Crelon's protege after all. If she complained about me to him, I'd better be writing my resume and sending it to other people.

I sat down feeling depressed again. I knew she scored and I hated it.

Dorian went on with her work. Then the door opened and the Oxford group entered with Michel.

"Ah, Dorian," Michel said with a big voice. "Here are our guests."

She looked around and I watched her turn on her smile. The men stared at her with some admiration. This was after all, the quintessential French woman. Elegant, thin and fashionably put together. I noticed Dorian wore spiked heels today. Usually she wore something more comfortable. She was almost thirty years old. Her degree was within reach - her PhD - which was going to point her into the

stratosphere of research somewhere -
perhaps Oxford?

The introductions were made and
the men mingled with her. Michel
would utter a laugh in between
comments. Dorian was clearly their
curiosity. I wasn't happy that she
could merely smile and make men her
slave. I decided to go about my work.

Michel managed to glance at me.
Finally while the others consulted
Dorian on her own project, Michel
called to me and said, "Agnes, we
think that a nice group dinner would
be good. I'll leave it to you to make
arrangements for a nice dinner.
Nothing too expensive," he looked over
at Dr Sydnor who flashed a cautious
look at him. I guessed the Oxford

Team was not into lavish meals. I laughed inwardly at this.

"Yes, of course, Dr. Crelon," I said respectfully. "I'll make arrangements. What would be a good time for us all to go for dinner?"

"Oh, let's say - "

"We can have an early dinner," interjected Dr Sydnor. "We've been up since dawn today."

Michel's smile dimmed. "Of course." He turned to me and said, "How about five o'clock this afternoon? Somewhere nearby. We don't want them to have to take a taxi."

"I know just the place," Dorian chimed in. The men looked at her expectantly. "How about *Le Cygne*?"

Dr Sydnor looked horrified. He had heard of *Le Cygne*. "No that's way too expensive. We are after all on an expense account."

Dorian lost her smile.

Michel looked at me for a suggestion. There was a mute plea in his eyes.

I drew a breath. "There's small bistro named Alexandre near here. It's really quite good."

"Ok, good," Michel clapped his hands. "Let's go now and find our places in the conference room. You have your slides ready?"

"We have our slides, yes." Mike said, his eyes on Agnes with a smile.

"Good," Michel ignored Dorian who faded away into her own world.

"I'll see you ladies in twenty minutes, shall I?" Michel asked without expecting a response. He herded them all out as Renee came in, her hands full of bags of pastry that were to be served at the conference.

"Damn it," Dorian said coolly. "I wanted *Le Cygne*."

"It's too expensive. Even the big fellow knew it."

Renee figured out what happened. "*Le Cygne* - so elegant. Love their food," she remarked. "Here let's get the pastries ready. I've got a stash of paper plates near the sink cupboard. Dorian can you get them for me?"

Dorian looked at Renee with incredulity. "You want ME to fetch these stupid paper plates?"

Renee smiled. "Yes please. You're much taller than either me or Agnes. Do it now then we can go and make the table arrangement."

Dorian stamped her way to the cupboard and took out a carton that held the party plates. I said very little but enjoyed this hugely.

Chapter Three

I almost came late to the Oxford
group's presentation because of a
problem in my experiment. When I got
there, almost all the seat were taken.
I searched for a chair to sit in and
found one near the front. When I got
to the chair I realized that one of
the men from Oxford was sitting next

to me. I glanced at his face and he was looking up at me. We smiled at each other then I put on my formal face and took my notepad and pen to listen and take notes.

"How are you?" asked the man from Oxford. I'd forgotten his name.

"Fine," I whispered back.

"What's your name again?" He asked, ignoring the speaker who was droning on about something to do with electrophoresis.

"I'm Agnes. Agnes Dumont."

"Oh, that's right." He said with a gentle tone. "I'm Ronan Michaels."

I nodded, "Yes, I remember."

The speaker looked at us and cleared his throat. Ronan said nothing but gazed up at the speaker

who was the wobbly looking fellow.
"Is there anything wrong?" Asked the
speaker.

"Nothing. Nothing at all."
Ronan smiled at him with an affable
expression in his face.

"Good." Spoke the man sharply.
"I'll move on."

Somewhere in the back I knew a
few people were noticing that I'd been
talking out of turn. I tried to
ignore the warmth that my face started
to feel. Ronan merely lounged in his
chair and I could tell he wasn't
attending this talk.

The topic was boring to me but
that was the usual problem with these
presentations. I started to think how
my career in science was not going

anywhere. It might have depressed me then but I realized this path I had was adequate enough to keep me employed and gave me the means to see my therapist. I also had enough money to pay for my rent, and the food and the clothes that I had to wear. I also thought of how lucky I was to live in Paris. I was not a Parisian by birth, but when I went to college in Paris I loved it well enough to settle down in this City of Lights.

I didn't realize that the speaker had finished until the crowd erupted in applause. There were a few of the group that asked some questions. I felt rather stupid not knowing what the man spoke about. I was lucky I thought that I didn't have to take a quiz about this man's presentation.

There was a lull in the group
while people started to drift away.
The man beside me sat behind and
looked at me speculatively. "By the
way, I'm really hoping you could tell
me what the best place here to go for
Japanese food?"

I stared at him. "Japanese
food?"

"You eat that here, don't you?"

"I - er - yes, we do."

"I'd like it if you could take me
to a Japanese restaurant. I'll pay
for your food of course."

"Oh, that would be fine," I
stammered. "I hadn't thought you'd
want to eat Japanese food."

"No, I like but I don't get it

much where I work."

"I'd be happy to take you to a Japanese restaurant." I smiled at him feeling quite happy. This man was interesting to me now.

He smiled back and I saw he had a slight dimple on his cheek when he smiled. "What about if I met you later somewhere right around here?"

I said, "Yes, outside this door, is that what you were thinking?"

"Yes." He replied with a sober look in his eye.

"I'm sure that will be fine."

"What time do you think we can meet?"

I glanced at my watch. "What about half past four o'clock?"

"That's good."

"What will you do now?" I asked, not wanting for us to part ways.

He shrugged. "I think I could do with a walk. I have to check on my hotel and then I'll be back to talk to your boss."

"Oh."

"I'll be working here someday. I think it's good to work with Crelon, don't you think?"

"He's one of the foremost scientists in the field."

"I'm really not that up on his main area of expertise. Which I think it would be good if I knew more of it."

"What do you work on?"

"I work on something rather obscure." He laughed.

I wondered if he was being coy. "What is it? Is it something new and undiscovered?"

"Something like that." He seemed unwilling to talk about it.

"Will you have a presentation about it this week?"

"Yes I will." He got up finally. "I must get back to my hotel. I'll see you half past four, then?"

I got up as well. "Yes of course."

He left but not before I noticed he was quite tall and slim, with broad shoulders. He was dressed in a jacket with a pair of chinos and moccasins. I thought he looked quite attractive. I hugged my notepad to myself and wondered whether he was married.

"Are you coming back to the lab?"
Renee's voice boomed at me from the
side of the room.

I started and then smoothed my
sweater with a hand. "I'm going
back."

She looked at me closely from
where she stood. "Seems like you've
got yourself a friend," she remarked.

"I was being helpful. Isn't that
what I'm supposed to do?"

Renee said nothing. She left the
room and I followed her back to the

lab slowly.

The time until I was to meet
Ronan went rather slowly. Once or
twice I ventured out of the lab in
order to catch a glimpse of him. He
was interesting. I thought it could
be nice if we did have something to
eat together. I might learn something
about Oxford and he would learn about
Paris. He seemed to be comfortable in
traveling. But he wasn't that
impressed with his colleague, which
amused me. I wondered whether he'd be
given a look from his superior for
talking in the meeting. Or they'd
already taken him for granted. Oxford
researchers weren't all serious,
perhaps, I thought.

I was about to finish my work
when Dorian entered. She went
straight for me and said, "I hear
you're to take some of them out for a
dinner thing. I'd like to come
along."

"Oh, no, I'm not. I'm er - taking
one of them out but you could take the
others out for dinner." I said
blithely, trying to keep my face from
falling. I hated her for interfering.
Why did she make me so irate for
being?

She pondered this. "Oh, so one
of them's going with you?"

"Yes."

"Which one?"

I tried to grasp at some thought

that would discourage more questions. "I'm taking that man Ronan whathisname."

She raised an eyebrow. "Which one was that guy?"

"He's the one in the blue navy suit," I replied.

She frowned. "Oh." Then she pursued the topic. "What - where are you going to take him?"

"He wanted to go to a Japanese place."

She made a face. "Yech, I hate Japanese food."

She left after that and I almost slumped in my chair in relief.

The time came when my guest would come to have me take him to a Japanese restaurant. It was four o'clock in the afternoon. Then, it dawned on me that I did not know any Japanese restaurants in the area.

I quickly got up from my desk where I was dawdling and went to the telephone which stood next to the large Paris phone directory. I jostled another book next to it and caused a slight commotion.

It was enough to get Renee's attention. She was applying lipstick with her hand mirror. "What is it you're looking for, Agnes?" She asked.

"I don't have any idea where a Japanese restaurant is in this area. Do you?"

I riffled through the telephone

book. There was the section of
restaurants which took up a quarter of
the book.

"I surely don't know." Renee said
with a bored tone.

The door opened and admitted
Michel with his Oxford Group.

"There you are, my ladies,"
Michel said with a flourish. "Here's
our group raring to feast on the
Parisian foodscape."

"Agnes is already getting me to a
Japanese restaurant." Ronan
volunteered.

"Is that so?" Dr Sydnor asked,
his eyebrows raised. "I'm not quite
that brave with Japanese cuisine."

Ronan came to my side. "I'm sure
we'll be fine, won't we Agnes?"

I nodded but gave him a look.
"I'm afraid I don't know any Japanese
restaurants in the area. Here's the
telephone book. We should find
something good here."

Ronan took me by the arm. "No,
put on your jacket and let's get out
of here. I'm betting these very good
taxi drivers will know where to find a
Japanese restaurant."

I let the book slide out of my
hand and followed him out the door.

I heard only the sounds of Renee
who was being quizzed by the remaining
members of the Oxford group.

Ronan was in good spirits. He
seemed to be one of those people who

didn't let the foreignness of a city
daunt him. We took the elevators down
and then once we were outside the door
of the building, he took my hand
firmly and we went to the curb where
by magic a taxi came to rest in front
of us.

"That's good, how did that
happen?" I exclaimed.

"Get in," he said excitedly.

We got inside the taxi. Ronan
gave a fairly good version of his
French to the cab driver. He said he
wanted to go to a Japanese restaurant
and he was willing to go out of the
area we were in. "Oh, of course," the
taxi driver smiled with a nod. He put
the car in gear and sped away from the
curb.

Ronan settled back next to me and smiled. "I'm raring for something good. Do you like sushi?"

"Yes I like it." I lied.

"That's amazing." He looked at me with wonder in his eyes. "How did you cultivate a taste for sushi?"

"I don't know. I think when I was in university a few of my classmates liked to visit a Japanese restaurant. But that was a long time ago."

He looked at me consideringly. "You look like you still could be a uni student. How old are you?"

I drew back slighty. He was being too forward. Nobody ever asks a woman for their age in Paris. "Ah - I'm twenty five."

Ronan nodded. "I'm twenty-
eight."

I felt rather glad he said that,
even though the topic daunted me.
"I'm surprised you're only twenty-
eight."

"Why's that?"

"I don't know - you've a great
deal of knowledge already - I think
that's because you are from Oxford.
Such a lot of smart people there."

"I was on full scholarship when I
was working on my DPhil."

"DO you like it where you're
working?"

"No, not specially."

"Is it not exciting to work in
Oxford?"

"No." He tried to stifle a yawn.

Clearly the subject matter was boring
him. "We have about the same type of
things in the laboratory that yours
has. I often forget that I'm in
Oxford when I'm doing my work. I'm
from another city in England. Have
you heard of York?"

"I have. But nothing more than
the name."

He watched the view that we
passed. The Eiffel Tower loomed over
us. It was sometimes closer to us and
then with a turn of the wheel of the
cab the Tower receded in the
background. We drove over the Pont
Neuf Bridge. There were several
seagoing vessels below on the water.
The sun was still high and there were
a good number of people who walked the

sides of the streets.

"I'm really eager to find another job. I have only some weeks left on my fellowship."

"Where will you go?"

"I'm not quite sure yet."

"You must be sending your resumes to all the places where you might get interviewed."

"That isn't quite what I'm doing. I'm thinking of working for a different scene altogether."

He became more interesting to me. "What scene are talking about?"

"I'm bored, Agnes." Ronan said, quietly. "It's a boring job being a researcher. Oxford is teeming with research people. But nobody is that happy. I don't relish working in a

laboratory where people are scarce.
Nobody to really talk to. I don't
like dealing with plates of plastic,
and test tubes and machines. Objects,
that is all they are."

"What about your research? It's
got to be exciting to be part of Dr
Sydnor's group?"

I worried about his attitude. I
thought that scientific research was
one of the best things one could do.

"My research will continue under
someone else. I don't care about it."

He seemed so final in his
statement. He looked outside the
window and watched the beautiful
scenes we passed. "Now, I wouldn't
mind living in Paris. How long have
you lived here, Agnes?"

"I've been here since I was a
child. My parents lived in another
city in the South of France. Then my
father decided to try the city life.
He was a farmer and my mother's health
was delicate. So we moved to Paris. He
was still young enough to become an
apprentice to a grocer. We had a rich
relative who gave us a place to live."

"That's good. I think farming is
tough." He said. "I lived in
Yorkshire. Many farmers there, and I
was one of those who was a farmer's
son." A smile crinkled the corners of
his eyes. "We are almost the same -
the children of farmers. How
interesting."

I wondered at that statement. He
seemed so easy to get to know. Not

the sort of Englishman I had envisioned, someone who was open with his words. There seemed to be no real reason for him to hide anything about himself. I settled back and decided to enjoy the evening with Ronan.

Chapter Four

We arrived at the Japanese restaurant and with a bit of good fortune we were given a table almost immediately. Michael didn't want the tables where people curled up with socked feet. We sat at the conventional tables, which suited me well.

The waiter left us to study our menus. I was not that conversant with Japanese food. But Ronan seemed to know what he wanted. Finally, he put the menu down and announced, "I'll have one of everything."

We laughed at that. I decided on something that was cooked and not raw. It wasn't a problem for me to eat sushi but with all that was happening in the world it was best to err on the side of safety.

We had a hot bowl of miso soup and Ronan had a large tray of sushi of different types and colours. I settled of a dinner box which had fried vegetables and shrimp and a bed of vinegar rice. We talked for some

time. Nothing that was too heart
opening as what he said in the cab.

"I suppose you should at least
taste one of these lovely things," he
motioned to a lovely piece of sushi.
"It's got tuna and some roe in it. Try
it."

I hesitated.

He pushed over a small bowl that
had a green dab of something in it
swimming in soy sauce. "You take the
sushi and then you dip it into this
sauce. The green thing is called
wasabi. It keeps the raw taste down.
Go on."

I let myself have the sushi and
gave it a nice bath in the wasabi-
sauce and ate it. The flaring
spiciness of the wasabi made a great

impression on my palate and my nasal passages. "Oh my!" I exclaimed.

"Go on it's good," Ronan said smiling and then chuckling at my reaction. "I'd be glad to take your picture as you eat it. You really are a naive girl."

"When it comes to sushi," I retorted, wiping my eyes with a napkin.

"Ok, never mind, lesson's over."

"I'm not sure I like being schooled." I said coolly.

He threw me a questioning glance and then picked out another piece of sushi and popped it into his mouth after letting it get washed in the potent wasabi-soy sauce mixture.

We sat companionably as the world

outside went from the light of day
into the dusk.

"What about you, are you
finishing a degree, Agnes?" He asked
suddenly.

"No, I'm not."

"Why not? Will you be a
technician forever?"

"Not sure why technician isn't a
good thing to be forever."

"Oh, so Michel gives you some
acknowledgements in his papers?"

"I have a small thank you at the
bottom of his papers. If I work with
him on something." I felt a bit
defensive.

"But don't you wish you could do
more? Perhaps finish an advanced
degree? A Masters would be the next

step. Where did you finish your BA?"

I decided to be honest. "I finished at the *Lycée*. I didn't much care to go on. The subject matters weren't appealing."

"But what if you were to work for something more - a bigger company - like that big pharmaceutical company?"

"No."

"No?" He leaned back and took a slug of his Asahi beer. "I'm sure it's all ok. I have a PhD in Biochemistry. But I'm not happy with it. I don't like working in a lab. I guess it's really just curiosity asking you why you're not as into getting a better degree."

I leaned back as well and looked at him directly. "If you're a PhD and

you're bored, why do I want to pursue
something higher than my degree now?"

"So what do you like to do when
you're not working?"

I paused. "I - I guess I go home
and take care of my home, I have a pet
cat. I'm really rather a homebody.
I'm not that interested in doing
anything more than what I do at work."

"But why?" He looked sadly at me.
"This is Paris. So many lovely things
to do here. Don't you even do the
museums?"

I made a face. "Museums aren't
my kind of fun."

"So what about boyfriends?"

"I have none."

Michael was quiet for a while. "I
wish you said you had."

"Oh, and why is that?"

"Just because I am feeling sorry for you. All you do is work for eight hours a day and then you go home to your cat."

It sounded ridiculous to my ears how he summed up my life. It made me almost burst into tears. "I don't just do that. I am in therapy. I've been depressed for some years."

The look in his face made me realize he was terribly affected by my honesty. "Oh."

"Yes." I tried not to look too noble. It was a matter of fact. People I knew were aware of my mental health and how it was making it difficult to do much more than get to work and then take care of the house.

"Why are you depressed?"

"I -" I tried to stop the catch in my voice. "I had a love affair."

"Oh." The tone in his voice made it clear he summed it up in his mind as something that made a great deal of sense. "What happened to you and him? He left you or what?"

"You are too nosy, Ronan."

"No, I do care."

"Good heavens." I tried to look for the waiter to order another drink.

He motioned for the waiter to come. "Another drink for the mademoiselle, please." Ronan said without an emotion to his voice.

"I think we don't know each other well enough to tell you what happened."

"Bullshit." He said coolly.
"I'm here and I want to know because I
think you should be happy and pursue
all kinds of opportunities. Get that
bastard out of your mind and do
something else to show everyone he's
not anyone to hang your hopes on.
He's gone, is he? Left for some
woman?"

I nodded. "Yes. I think it was a
bad relationship looking back on it.
He was English too."

Ronan looked pained. "Oh my.
That's not good. I'm not the sort you
want to know then, is that what you
might think?"

"I think you should be a
psychiatrist, Ronan. You seem to be
good at drawing people out with your

words." I smiled tremulously. "I
wonder whether they have some other
afters to take? I think this meal is
not quite satisfying to me."

"Why don't we go get some
dessert?" He asked. He told the
waiter that they would take the bottle
of beer with them. "We're leaving.
Give us the bill." Ronan told the
waiter who went away looking puzzled.

We looked at each other and then
we giggled. "You are silly." I said
finally. "If you are English and that
bastard I fell for is English, I think
both of you must have been born on
different coasts."

"What was he all about?"

"Rich, belonged to some noble
family, had everything - an apartment

in the Rue Nord, I was one of his
girls. I found out too late I was
only one of a group of women he went
through."

"Ah. That sounds about right.
These tosh people." Ronan smiled
mirthlessly. "What was his name?"

"Paul Trent."

"Oh. It doesn't ring a bell."
His words were said almost too
casually. I detected something beneath
his words. As though he fished out
something that he prized. I glanced
at him and saw his face was in repose,
as though he was tucking this
information in his memory for review
later.

We went out and walked at length.

The long shadows of dusk fell over us.
It was of no importance to us. The
bustle of the streets, the Place de la
Concorde was somewhere ahead, lights
were everywhere. If there were stars
in the sky they were not visible
because the lights in Paris
overshadowed them.

He walked fast and so I had to
keep up with him. He was tall, about
six feet and I wasn't. But I was able
to keep up and then we went into a
small place where they served
pastries. He and I went into a corner
table and someone took our order.

We said very little in the way of
importance. He asked me about my cat.
Then we talked about his presentation
that he was to give in the morning.

Then his place back in Oxford. I was
a bit hesitant to ask him about his
personal life. I didn't know why but
it seemed as though he wasn't about to
talk about it. I was disappointed but
it might have been too soon for me to
ask. I wasn't sure about it but this
man was a mixture of attitudes. He
seemed more preoccupied. So I let it
go and decided he wasn't going to be a
regular fixture at the lab after he
and his group left.

It made me feel somehow
disappointed. I did not wish to feel
more than that. He was not that
handsome. Not like Paul was handsome.
Paul had fair hair, blue eyes and
delicate hands. This man Ronan had
the hands of someone who might have

been a pugilist, and his build was deceptively slim - he was sparely built but when he would flex his arms the muscles appeared under his tweed jacket. His face was somewhat obscured by a three-day shadow - dark curling hair covered his head and his eyes were grey and quite intelligent. Perhaps that might have been why I wasn't attracted to him at first. The shadow of my past affair with Paul was making it difficult to see any man as comparable to him and thus make me forget about Paul altogether.

We finished our dessert. I felt rather giddy. "I'm quite dizzy." I said suddenly.

"What? Why?"

"I think that I've had a bit too

much sugar."

He laughed at me. "Oh, you
Parisian women. You are too thin,
Agnes. What about if we sat here for
a few minutes and then we can go find
a cab and take you home?"

We stayed for a few minutes as he
suggested. But the dizziness was
still there. "I'm sure it will pass."
I kept saying.

"Are you diabetic or what?" He
asked.

"No."

"Healthy enough?"

"Yes, I'm very healthy."

"Well, how far is it from your
apartment?" He asked, as if deciding
on something.

"I think it's about twenty

minutes away."

"Good, let's walk there, I think
the cool air will keep you from
falling over in a coma."

"Good idea." I said with a
smile.

We walked hand in hand, mostly
because I was truly unsteady. I
wondered why I felt dizzy but that was
a memory by the time we had made a
quarter of the walk home.

We arrived at my place and
realized simultaneously that we had
spent a long evening together. I
hesitated to invite Ronan up and
thankfully, he said, "I think it's
better for me to get back to my hotel.
I'll see you tomorrow, ok?"

"Ok," I smiled up at him. His smile was kind and cheerful.

"I had a lovely evening, Agnes. Your city is as always so very magical."

"It is, isn't it?" I felt as though this was something I've forgotten. "Living here I've gotten used to its magic."

"Don't let that pass you by."

Something in his words touched me and I was lifted up in spirit by them.

We parted at the bottom of the steps that led to my apartment.

I decided not to watch him leave. He seemed capable of getting to his hotel, so I went up and opened my door.

The door revealed the same cosy

place that I had left it in the
morning. Somehow I felt as though I
was visited by someone that drew me
out of myself. I was quite full from
the dinner and pastry so I went on to
settle for the night.

As I lay in bed that night, I
smiled to myself and thanked God for a
good day.

Chapter Five

Getting to work was a mess the
next morning. The presentation of the
Oxford Group was to continue that day.
Ronan's turn was up. I was impatient
with the Metro and for that day the

train was slow as it ever had been. I
was dressed in a more presentable
outfit - something from Agnes B and
then a cardigan sweater from the same
designer. I had on a pair of shoes
that were still comfortable but
presentable for the day. I thought
that Dorian's outfit yesterday was
very fashionable but I didn't wish to
compare mine with hers. She earned a
good deal more money due to her
position as a postdoctoral scientist.
I tried not to think of her as I took
my place in the Metro train.

By the time I arrived, the
laboratory was already busy. There
wasn't a chance to get a croissant
from the cafe. Renee was nowhere to
be seen, so I assumed she was already

making preparations to serve some sort of breakfast for the group.

There were many who sat in the conference room and I took a seat in the back, momentarily pausing by the small table where sweets and coffee were on display. I forgot my notepad so I decided to enjoy the presentation.

Ronan wore a suit today and his presentation was understandable. Some questions were asked which interrupted his talk, but he took them good naturedly. I wondered whether he had any qualms of speaking to a crowd. He was very impressive and his data was quite credible. Michel watched from part way in the back. Dorian sat in the front, dolled up in her newest outfit that I hadn't seen before. Clearly she'd decided he was someone to impress. She also asked a few questions, which I thought seemed to be contrived.

Renee was also present and her face was impassive. She fidgeted with her pen and wrote little in her notepad. A few other scientists expressed interest in Ronan's work.

Ronan didn't look at my direction. I decided he'd forgotten about our dinner last night. I wasn't too disappointed but I kept my feelings under cover. It wouldn't do to think much of a 'first' date. It wasn't really a date. What would Dr. Prince say to that? My mind wandered a bit, and then finally the

presentation was over. People were
still interested and asked more
questions at the end.

Dr Sydnor rose to help Ronan
answer the questions. It was somewhat
obvious that Ronan found is sharing
the podium somewhat of a distraction.
Then I saw Ronan let Dr Sydnor take
over and include Michael's work in the
greater aim of the Oxford Group's
larger vision.

Michel finally got up and said to
Ronan in front of the group: "I'm
very impressed by your work, Ronan. I
wonder if you and Dorian here could
have some time together and she can
pick your brains about it?"

Dorian was in her glory and she
beamed with pleasure. Ronan looked at

Dorian and said, "Of course. We're all here to learn, aren't we?"

Somehow his head moved slightly as if to take a look at the audience. I wondered whether he was searching for me. I quelled that idea and got up with the rest of the audience to return to our laboratories.

As I walked to our laboratory, I saw Ronan and Dorian make their way to one of the conference rooms reserved for consultations. Renee came to my side. "I'm happy we've had a successful morning, aren't you?"

"Yes, it was a good presentation."

"He and you went out last night, didn't you?"

"Yes, we did." I wasn't sure whether I wanted to discuss it.

"How did it go?"

"I think we had a good evening. We went to a Japanese restaurant."

Renee paused. "He wanted to go there? That's different." Then after a moment, she said, "Oh, I remember. You were looking for a Japanese restaurant in the phone book."

"He's not someone you could predict, I think."

"Any idea if he wants you to go out again with him?"

"Renee, really, I was merely showing him some of the city." I tried to increase my steps away from her to avoid any more of her inquisitiveness.

"I guess that's just how it is."
Renee sighed. "I was hoping you'd get
his attention."

We had gone into our laboratory
by the time she said this. I turned
to her and said, "You are so romantic
all of a sudden."

"I'm not happy you're staying out
of the dating scene, Agnes. You are
still attractive. You need to find
another man to make your life
interesting."

I hated her words but inside I
wasn't too unhappy to think someone
wanted me to be happy. What was happy
however? I tried not to think too
much about it. Like everything else
that touched me personally I didn't
want this topic to occupy my thoughts.

Later on, Renee took up her lab
coat and put it on. "I'll be busy in
the cold room. If you need me I'll be
there."

"Fine."

"I think Crelon said the group
was going to go and find their own
place to eat today. They won't be
bothering us much. They have a
schedule today to meet other important
scientists in the building. You
probably won't see Michael again."
Her voice took on a rather Delphic
prophetic tone.

"I'm sure that will happen." I
tried to mask the rising tension in my
voice. "I'll be quite busy with all
the stuff I'm doing in my project."

"I'll see you later, then."

As the day went on I hardly saw
Ronan. There wasn't a clue where he
could be at any moment. Dorian was
not anywhere either. She came and
went at her own leisure. Her work was
not that pressing these days, as she
was in the process of reviewing her
data in order to write a paper about
it.

I went on with my work, trying to
keep the evening before under my
consciousness. I wanted to look good
that day and it seemed as though not
even Renee said anything about my
outfit.

In a fit loneliness, I decided to
take a walk outside. I took nothing
with me, not even my coat. I got off
the elevator and left the building. I

wandered off to get away from the thoughts that beset me. I didn't want to be one of those women who would start weaving ideas just after one evening with an eligible man.

I was able to get out of the stressful thoughts and instead found myself window shopping. The laboratory was in the same area as the shops that sold clothes and cosmetics. I felt better. The weather was cold, actually chilly. I didn't mind it at all. It kept my from thinking of sad thoughts.

I was out of the laboratory for an hour. That was going to have to count as my lunch hour, I knew. Renee was not one to notice but I knew enough about how work days went.

It was late afternoon when I returned to the laboratory. When I got to the door, I happened to see Ronan and his group leaving and getting into a taxi. I felt let down. It was almost as though I'd never see him again. Like a dejected child who missed out on a treat, I went up to the lab using the stairs. Each step made me feel heavier and by the time I got out of the stairwell, and into the hall where I had my laboratory I was filled with a heaviness in my body.

Crelon found me as I was entering my laboratory. "Hi, Agnes, what about if you talked to Dr Sydnor about your project? They were discussing something that I think you might be interested in."

"Oh, that sounds like a good idea." All the heaviness in my body left me. I felt so happy all of a sudden. "Tell me where to talk to him."

"I've asked Lizette to set up a meeting with you and Dr Sydnor. It will not be until later today. You can stay, can't you?"

"Of course!" I fairly sailed into the lab and felt quite hungry. I was so excited and felt as though I was blessed by a fairy who was watching my progress. Something to tell my therapist, I thought. Then I realized I wouldn't see him for another two weeks. I was the picture of industriousness that afternoon. It was so exciting to be recognized for my work.

Later I received an email from
Lizette, Crelon's secretary, giving me
an appointment to meet Dr Sydnor for a
half hour of consultation. I kept
this close to my heart, even though I
wanted to sing it to anyone who was
close by. Even Renee, who came by,
didn't notice how I was feeling. She
merely sighed and bowed her head over
her lab notebook.

Chapter Six

The next day of the meeting with
the Oxford group, I ran into Dorian
and we had an awful row. She saw me
enter the laboratory and a strange
smile came to her lips. "Ah, just the

person I wanted to see."

"What do you want?" I asked, sensing myself get tense. I hadn't even put my jacket down and already she was aiming for an attack.

"I'm wondering whether you know what happened to that enzyme I've put away - the one that I am getting ready to do my experiment with." Dorian got out of her chair and started towards me.

Renee looked at us apprehensively. But she said nothing.

"I'm not sure I know what you mean, Dorian," I said, heading for my desk and removing my coat. "What enzyme? Where would it be?"

"I've put it in my part of the freezer. Now I can't find it."

"Sorry, I don't know what its called. What do you call it? I have not seen anything at all."

"It's called Fibrozyme. It will be used to make a definitive step in my research." She started to raise her voice. "It will get me out of here and into the Salk institute in california, where it will be heaven!"

I looked at her coolly. "I'm not sure I have seen this Fibrozyme thing you are stashing away. Our shelves are on different parts of the freezer. You have to find it somewhere else, not with me."

I made a move to sit down and as soon as I did this, Dorian came at me. I ended up sitting on the floor, feeling dazed.

Renee came over finally and helped me up. "Don't you dare help her up!" Dorian said with a fulminating look at me.

Just then Crelon entered and saw the carnage. "Hey, what's going on?"

Dorian beat me to it. She accused me of stealing her precious Fibrozyme, and that she was having it out with me and I hit her.

"That's a damn lie!" I said passionately. "I've no idea where this enzyme is and she's terribly wrong about everything."

Crelon's face tautened. "I won't have any violence in this laboratory." He looked at Renee. "What happened, Renee?"

She didn't say anything. I

realized Dorian had something over
Renee as well. "I'm sorry." Renee
said finally.

Dorian went on embellishing her
accusations at me. How I never
respected her, never gave her any help
when she needed it, and definitely
mocked her superiority over me. I
watched this with dawning realization
that she wanted me to leave the
laboratory forever.

I looked at Crelon. He was
listening to her. I felt sick. What
is happening to me? I asked myself.
"I'm innocent." I said to Crelon.
"She's terrible to me."

Crelon looked at me and said,
"Come into my office. Let's talk."
That tone of his voice made it

clear he was going to favor Dorian's side.

I marched into his office right after him. He went in and didn't close the door. The staff outside might have heard this too.

"She's very high strung." He said to me. "Don't take this the wrong way but if you can't get along with her, you really can't stay."

I froze. "What?"

"You'll have to leave, Agnes."

His face was implacable. He steepled his fingers and then thought the better of it. "I'll give you a good reference. But you'd best leave."

I said nothing to that. "If you say so. I'll be taking off."

Warring thoughts in my head were
arguing whether I should have fought
for my job. Then I realized that
Dorian had him under her spell. I
wasn't in the same league as Dorian.
She was a glamor girl, someone who
could attract a great deal of
financial support because she was
pretty, good in the ways of talking up
the projects and an asset. I wasn't an
asset as I realized. I had no real
ambition in the world of scientific
research. My affair with Paul put
that to bed. I no longer had that
urge to do great things because love
had left.

I spoke slowly. "I'm taking it
that you're firing me?"

Crelon frowned. "No, don't do

that. I'll give you notice you're
leaving. Say that you're in need to
training. Go to school, get another
degree. I'll give you severance pay.
Just don't make a scene. The oxford
group will hear of this and I don't
want it."

I looked at him with dislike.
"Ok, I'll do what you say." There was
nothing else I could do.

As I walked out of the
laboratory, I saw Ronan who was
looking at something with Dorian. I
felt ill at the sight. She was going
after him as well. What a horrible
little tart, I thought of Dorian.

I passed them. Ronan looked up

at me. "Hey, how are you?"

Dorian looked at me coldly. "Listen, we've got to discuss this news soon."

"Oh, sure." Ronan saw my face and his mien took on a concerned expression. "I'll be with you in a while." He went to me. "What's wrong?"

Dorian fairly stamped her feet in disgust. She was shooting daggers at me. I felt them as though they were real. "Look nothing. I'm leaving. I have to find some other place to work."

"Hell, really?" Ronan asked. He looked puzzled. "Ok, well, I want to see you for lunch. Can we meet at the same place for lunch?"

"No, I can't."

"Sure you can."

"Ok, I'll be there." I didn't look at the time.

"I'll be your friend. Don't worry."

"Go back to Dorian. She's not happy you're talking to me."

"Damn that woman. Ok, I need to leave you." A thought came to mind. He seemed to read mine. "You better show up."

"And you better show up." I said meaningfully.

"I will."

I was just about to leave the building when Dorian caught up with

me. "You, I want to talk to you!"
Her voice rang out and some people who
were standing by stared.

I turned around and looked at
her. She wasn't that tall but she had
an advantage over me in height. "What
is it? I've left. You have no wish
to talk to me."

She was fairly steaming. "I want
you to stop seeing that man, Ronan.
Do you hear me?"

I hated her even more. "I'm
sorry he wanted to see me. If that's
all, good bye."

She stared at me and then she
flounced off. It was a small triumph
that she couldn't answer me. I
laughed and went out the door.

Chapter Seven

The streets of Paris were chilly
and the cold air blew against my
cheeks. I felt good strangely enough.
I was free of that job, and that woman
and the fake Renee. I had no job yes,
but it wouldn't be long before another

job would come up. A niggling thought
came to me and said that I would never
be good at anything. I hated to think
of it. I walked briskly and nodded
and smiled at the other pedestrians.

It was after ten in the morning.
I didn't know where to go after a
brisk walk that took out the tension
that I was feeling. I was not that
sad yet, because the exchange with
Dorian was all that I was going on and
how it made me feel good that Ronan
asked to see me again.

I sighed then and turned a corner
and found a small bakery and went
inside. Of the money I had in my
purse I spent half of it. I bought a

baguette and a wedge of cheese and
coffee. They had a small corner that
people sat in and so I sat down with
what I had. The morning's tension
made me feel hungry and tired.

As I ate the baguette and cheese,
I thought of calling my psychiatrist.
He was probably busy now, I realized.
But it would have to wait. I didn't
find much comfort in talking to him.
I thought of calling my friend ( ) and
yet her friendship was somewhat
unfulfilling. She had friends and a
lover. A gregarious woman, I knew. I
wasn't as friendly as her and my
number of friends were counted on one
hand.

I decided to enjoy the baguette.
I also went back to get a bottle of
water. I needed to take my anxiety
pill. It was all I could do. I was
grateful for it.

Lunchtime came along. I was
early. I'd been filled with the
baguette and cheese but the tension
that came in the morning made me still
peckish. I surveyed the menu and
noticed someone standing by my table.
It was Ronan.

"Hi," I said.

"Hi," said Ronan. He looked down
at me with a look of concern. He sat
down and ignored the menu. "Look,
I've heard this story that you were
belligerent."

"Oh," I scoffingly said. "I was
NOT beliigernt. Who told you that
lie?" I suddenly lost my appetite.
"Look, I'm really raring for some
Japanes food. I hope you're not going
to read me the riot act for being
fired."

He took his napkin and placed it
on his lap. The waiter was prompt.
"Did you wish to wait - I can come
back."

"Yes, I'd like to look at the
menu."

I studied Ronan surreptitiously
while I surveyed my own menu. He
looked exhausted. It seemed he had a
stressful morning.

We were quiet a moment or two.
"I'm sorry." Ronan looked up at the

menu. "I'm not sure that I can do
service to the menu."

"Will you let me order for you?
I know the sort of thing tht will help
a stress-laden stomach." I tried to
humour him.

He saw the humour and smiled, and
the lines of worry disappeared from
his forehead. "Look, I'm damned sorry
you left. I don't think they did this
fairly. I was told you had a row
with that Dorian woman. Is that
true?"

"She picked a row, not me."

"Ah."

"Yes, ah."

"So you were pushed out.
Whatever for?"

I was silent for a while. "I've

no idea, really. Dorian has been my thorn on the side. I think she's angling to be apart of your Oxford group. She's very ambitious."

"And so you saw through her?"

"I've worked with her in the same room for years now. She's tried everything to get to the top."

"No worries, it's not my problem."

"What do you mean?"

We noticed the waiter sidle by. "I think we should look at what we need to eat."

Ronan stretched his back and motioned for the waiter. "I'll have the combination box four. I'm also going to want a bottle of sake, please."

I raised my eyebrows. "A bottle? At this time of day?"

"I'm used to it. I like it. Would you share it with me?"

"I'm sure I'll like it. I have no job to return to. It's you that I'm worried about. You'll have to go back and face the same people."

He was quiet. He tried not to answer hastily. "Look, Agnes, I'm not sure I like what I saw today."

"You mean my sacking?"

"NO not just that. I saw some people angle to join the Oxford group, and that included Dorian. She wants heartily to go to England."

"Oh. Was that what was planned fo r me to do?"

He shook his head. "No, we wanted

to pick your brains, that's all."

"But she was obviously wanting to go with your research and perhaps find an excuse to visit Oxford?"

"Yes, that's about it."

"Damn. She's such a forward person, isn't she?"

He nodded. "There are many of those who think Oxford is the be-all and end-all."

The waiter took my order and swayed away. He looked forlornly at me. I sensed that he understood what we discussed in front of him.

"I'm sorry Ronan."

"Don't be. I have a notion that I won't be in Oxford for very long."

"Not because of me, I hope?"

"No, not only because of you.

It's been growing in my mind. I've seen many difficult situations at Oxford. Nothing to do with people, just the research. I'm thinking they have some problems getting funded and they're going with other groups, like Crelon's. These groups - well. . ."

"Oh, that is a common problem I heaer."

"Crelon's not that bad but I don't know much about him. Can you tell me what he's like?"

I paused because the sake came. We were given two small glasses. The sake was quite warm going down my gullet. "I'm not quite sure what you mean."

"Is he a good boss? What's he like when nobody's looking?"

"I can't say. I don't talk to him that much. He's like a bull in a china shop. Gets in the way. Lumbers in and out of the lab and shouting directions as he goes."

"Oh my."

"He's like that."

"You've not talked to him in private about your research?"

"Yes, I have. But these are just routine. Most of the time we have laboratory meetings. We don't do a lot of one to one discussions. Usually people are in the know about all that we're doing and so we all chip in with suggestions. And that's how it is."

"That's how it is here with us in Oxford."

"That's fine, isn't it?"

Ronan rubbed his curly head.
"I'm suspicious of that Dorian. I need
to talk to her later today. In
private. She and I have to discuss
this research that the Oxford team
wants to work on with Crelon."

"Not even with Crelon you're
talking to her?"

"No."

"I'd be wary but you can take
care of yourself, surely."

He grinned finally. "I'm not in
the mood to make love to a hussy who
made my friend leave in tatters. I
don't approve of it. Did Crelon side
with her, is that what happened too?"

"Yes." I looked down and tried
to control my emotions. I used to

think Crelon was my friend too. But
he felt that Dorian had more potential
to do well for his lab."

Ronan was not that happy to hear
that I could tell. "I'm sick of the
politics of scientific research."

"I am too."

The food came presently. We ate
heartily. Ronan and I ordered the
food that was warm and had a good
texture. We didn't eat sushi today.

"What will you do then?" Ronan
asked, in between chewing and having
his sake.

"I'll have to polish up my
resume. And send it to different
places."

"Not science again?"

"No, maybe. I don't know."

He looked concerned. "I'm sorry.
I might have influenced you. Not all
labs are like that, surely. Not here
in Paris."

"No, maybe." I said again.

We sat in silence finishing our
food. The sake was beginning to warm
my face and I felt somewhat fuzzy.
"I'm quite drunk, Ronan." I grinned
at him.

"No let's see, I'll order us some
coffee." He looked for the waiter.
"I don't see our waiter."

"He'll be by, soon enough."

"Go on and eat some more. Here,
have some more of my shrimp."

I reached over and took some of
his tempura shrimp. I love that
shrimp the way they cook them in

Japanese restaurants.

"I'm thinking I'll order some
more - what about you?" I asked.

"If that will keep you from
keeling over drunk, then go ahead,"
Ronan grinned back.

"It's too early for me to think
of working another job. I'm not that
old that I would be at a
disadvantage."

"No."

Chapter Eight

"I could go back to school," I
ventured shyly.

"That might be good. What will
you take?"

I sighed and said, "I can't tell.
I don't kow. I could go back and
studying nursing."

He gave a cry. "No, please no."

"Ok, then what do you suggest?"

"I don't know you very well.
What do you like to do in your spare
time?"

I was taken aback. I didn't have
much to do in my spare time.
"Nothing."

"Nothing?"

"Nothing."

"There must be something you can
do in your spare time."

"I can't think of it."

He looked worried. "Don't you
have any hobbies? Or maybe you could
- "

"What?"

"Could you work for a store as an
assistant?"

"A store?" The thought was almost a wild idea. I had not thought of working in a store. I thought of the little place that I passed going to my home. "I might go and ask around."

"That would help. You can't stay in your house feeling sad and dejected."

I felt somewhat better. Not another lab. Thank God. I do not wish to work in a lab anymore, I declared to myself.

"I'm going to have to tell my therapist about this," I muttered.

"Therapist?" He heard me.

"Yes," I cleared my throat, feeling embarrassed. "I'm seeing a therapist."

"Are you depressed or something?"

"I was. I had a bad affair. I was in hospital for a few weeks."

"Oh, poor dear."

He sounded so sympathetic.

"I'm alright now," I reassured him, biting into another shrimp.

"I'm sure he'll point you in the right direction. When will you see him?"

"Oh, not for a few weeks. I see him less and less. I guess I'm doing better." I shrugged and smiled at him, trying to look winning.

"Talk to him tomorrow. Or later after lunch. It's important he knows what happened today."

He looked at his wristwatch. "I'm due back in a half hour."

"Oh." I felt a wave of sadness.

He was so nice. It made it hard for me to think that I might never see him again after today.

He seemed to read my mind. Ronan regarded me closely. "Are you alright? Do you want me to see you later? I can remember where you live."

I felt a rush of happiness. "I'd like that, actually."

"Good. I'll come by. What's your cell phone number?"

He took out his cell phone and paused, to listen to me tell him my number. I gave it to him. He pocketed his cell phone and looked satisfied. "Look, that Dorian, I wouldn't worry about her. She's won this round. I know her type. Oxford's got lots of people like her."

I nodded. "It would be good if I had a different job. Laboratory work isn't my type of work it seems. It's too lonely."

"Don't go back to it. Even if that Crelon begs you to come back. Sydnor told me he said you were his top technician."

"Fat lot that helped me with Dorian."

"She's a bitch. Don't think about her now."

"I'm glad you're here, Ronan." I said simply.

He smiled again. It was so nice to have a friend finally, I thought.

We parted after a few minutes when he paid the bill. We turned to opposite sides of the street and he

went back and I went wandering through
the streets trying to keep that good
feeling that I received at lunch. A
full heart and a full stomach. I was
not sure I could say I was happy.
Some thoughts told me not to say it
out loud or even acknowledge it.

The cell phone rang and I took it
out of my pocket. It was Renee.

"What happened? Where are you?
I want to talk to you."

No, I'm not coming back. I don't
wish to discuss it with anyone."

"You need to go to the Human
Resources office. They need to have
you sign out." Her voice rapped
against my psyche. "It's de rigeur.
You need to have it all official. It
will help get you some recompense. The

government requires it from those who
have been fired."

The word "fired" made me wince.
"Oh, ok. But I won't go back now."
"Now, girl. Go back there and talk to
someone there."

"No, I'll call and make an
appointment. I'm not sitting there
looking to find the first person to
talk to."

"Stubborn girl. You won't find
another job in this area."

"I don't care Renee." I fairy
spat at her. "I wish you'd leave me
alone. I'll go now. Bye."

Good riddance, I said to myself.
I scowled all the way to the Metro and
then I decided t shake all of that bad
mood. I wish I could recover what I

had in my heart when Ronan and I were
in that restaurant together.

Chapter Nine

Sylvie was waiting by the fireplace and mewled when I got inside. I took off my coat and put my purse away. It was a very sad day after all. I went to put on some coffee and made a simple meal of soup. I went to the phone and dialed Mrs. Cortes' number.

"Hallo?" Said Mrs Cortes.

"Hallo, it's Agnes Dumont."

She remembered me. "Oh, *bonsoir,* how does it go?"

"I'm wondering would you like a person to help with your store? I lost my job today. Can I come and help?"

There was a pause. "Ok, you just called at the right time. My bakery needs someone to help. Can you come tomorrow at seven in the morning?"

Heavens, I said to myself. Seven? I swallowed and then responded, "Yes, I'll come then. Thank you!"

"Mind, we don't pay much. How much were you getting in that job?"

I told her. She said nothing at first. "I can pay you something but it won't be that much. We have a popular bakery so you could get something of a riase ina while."

"That is ok."

"Why did you lose your job?"

"I wasn't nice to the boss'
woman."

"Oh. That is stupid of that
bastard," she sniffed.

"I am glad you needed help. I'm
grateful."

"See you tomorrow. And knock on
the door and I'll come to open it. We
don't open until nine in the morning."

"I'll be there."

I sat with my bowl of soup and
talked to Sylvie.

"I'll be out of the house early

tomorrow Sylvie."

She said nothing but wiped her
face with a paw.

The doorbell rang presently and I
wondered who it might be. I went to
the door. "Who is it?" I asked aloud.

"It's Ronan."

I was surprised, pleasantly. I
opened the door and he came in. He
looked around before he walked into
the room. "What a surprise," I said
with a smile. "What happened? Di you
not go to work?"

"No, I decided to chuck work for
today."

He smiled amusedly at the cat who
was still washing her face. "Who's
she?"

"It's my cat, Sylvie. She's
rather a snob but since she didn't
leave the room, she could be happy
that you're here."

We went inside, after I shut the
door after him.

I wasn't sure what to say first.
Then I said, "And you are allowed to
leave. People do that of course, but
I'm surprised you chucked off work.
Are you alright?"

He shook his head. "No. Do you
have some more food to eat? I'm
famished."

"I have soup from the grocery
next door. I'll make you a bowl. Sit
and relax."

"I will." He sat at the table,
still watching amusedly my cat Sylvie.

"Sylvie, eh?" He bent down.   "Hi Sylvie."

Sylvie looked at him and then she mewed.

"What a sweetheart."

"She's a sweetheart."

"I'm due to have a chat with that Dorian. I don't much like the idea of telling he my recipes for a procedure. She's terribly inquisitive."

"I see."

"Well, she's like all the rest of them. They like Oxford so much they'll ask everything that we have in our library of methods and materials."

"She could easily get one of your papers."

"No it's not that. She wants me."

"Ah." I smiled ad then chuckled.
"Poor you. They love men who are so -
"

"So?" His eyebrow lifted.

I felt my cheeks redden. "Look,
Dorian recognizes you're one of those
favored sons of Oxford."

"Oh." He sounded disappointed.
"I thought you had an opinion of me
that I might like to hear. Spill it,
my dear Agnes."

I laughed finally. I was
surprised to hear myself laugh. I
hadn't laughed in a while.

"Ok, so you are sweet on me,"
Ronan said satisfactorily.

"You are a very good friend.
We've only met a few days ago. But
you are. Open and friendly."

"No I'm not always open and friendly. I"m rather a dour sort. Oxfod is a very businesslike place. Everyone is all about the work."

"I don't know. I see these shows on TV about Oxford and they all love a pint, don't they?"

He laughed. "Ok so we love a pint. You haven't one around do you?"

I said nothing but I shook my head.

"What if I went off to get us a few pints in a bottle or two?"

"I - ah - well, sure if you wish."

Ronan stood up and went to the fireplace where he stretched out his hands. "I think I'll have the soup first."

Chapter Ten

      I realized that I hadn't gone to
fetch him a bowl of soup. I went to
do that and gave him some bread as
well. He was still standing by the
fire when I placed his meal on the
table.

"How long have you stayed in this place?"

"Oh, since I was in college."

"It's nice. I like it."

"So do I. I got it from an old relative. She was sad that I hadn't had much to live on. I don't pay any rent but I do pay on the light and the gas. And some other things like internet."

"You are a self-sufficient girl."

"Is that something you don't approve of?"

"Oh, no, not really. Not at all."

"Come and have soup. It's good." I warmed up a bit more to him. "I've got a job."

He was amazed and went to the table to find his meal in front of him. "Tell me about it."

"I'll be the bakery assistant.
Next door. The lady who owns it said
they're in need of help. So I'll work
there."

"Interesting." He took some of
te soup. "This is rather good. What
on earth is it?"

"It's ah - well, I don't know
what they call it. Something like
beef stew but it has more vegetables."

"I like it."

"Yes, it's a nice thing they're
close by."

"I - "

The phone rang. We stared at
each other. Ronan said nothing but
kept eating.

I went to the phone. I

hesitated, feeling somehow a fear that it was something that I ought not to answer. I decided to throw my anxieties to the wind and answered the phone. "Hallo?"

It was Dorian. I felt a small shiver of fear and then I said, "Hello Dorian. What makes you call me?"

Ronan held up a hand as though to tell me not to tell her he was here.

"I'm looking for Ronan. Do you know if he's tried to contact you?" Her voice was peremptory.

"No he has not. If that is all -"

"You have to tell me if he comes by."

"Dorian, I'm sure you won't be first on my mind when and if he calls me."

"I hate that. You're such a
bastard."

"You are the most bastardly ever,
Dorian."

"I can't stand how you just left
us finally."

"You made that happen. Are you
trying to get me to come back?" I sat
back on my heels with a smile.

"NO!"

"Then we have nothing else to
talk about."

"Well, if you DO see him, tell
him I'm waiting for him. We had a
consultation to do this afternoon."

I said nothing.

"Did you hear me?"

"I heard you. If I do see him

I'll try to talk about nothing about
you. You're a sick woman, Dorian.
You need a lot of psychiatric help. I
hope you are happy with Michel."

I hung up with a snap and then
sighed loudly. "She gets me in such a
state." I said aloud.

"Soup is good. Can I have another
serving?"

"Of course." I took his bowl and
went to the stove where I ladled
another serving for him.

He sat looking a bit satisfied.
He accepted the second serving with as
much alacrity as he had the first one.
We sat in silence for some time. I
did not wish to spoil his meal by
speaking of a bastard like Dorian.

Sylvie jumped on the table and

Ronan looked surprised. "Does she do that?"

"I'm afraid she does. She won't want any food. Just wants to be sociable."

He looked a bit put off but then he kept eating. "I won't die from her company, I'm sure."

I laughed again. "You're very honest."

'That is why I'm not a happy man."

"Is it sad to work with Oxford group and seeing people all day that remind you of Dorian?"

"I'm immune to it but I do wish I'd had some other thing to do rather than put up with such a lot of people who are either too secretive and won't

spill what they're doing because
they're afraid I'll go up better than
them. Or, being too free with
themselves and boasting about their
latest accepted paper from some huge
journal. I'm disillusioned, Agnes."

Chapter Eleven

"Why not take a leave of absence,
a vacation or maybe change your area
of work?"

"That's something I've been
thinking of. But I'm afraid I'll see

the same types of people wherever I go to work. All of them groveling to become a big expert and write first author papers and travel to all parts of the world to spout off about their latest finds."

"But traveling is nice." I agreed with him but I did say this as a way to give him the other side of the question.

"I like to travel, yes."

"So."

"I'm not happy to travel only for work, however. And seeing the same old boobs wherever they might have their meetings."

"I think I'm sensing you aren't going to be an Oxford Group member for long."

"No." Ronan stretched and then reached up at Sylvie who liked him petting her. "She's a dear. Let me see, could I hold her?"

I was surprised but nodded.

"Here, kitty. What about a little hug? I need a hug."

Sylvie allowed him to take her into his arms. They made a lovely picture. A big man with a little cat in his arms.

Ronan looked at me with sheepish eyes. "I'm rather fond of you, Agnes. Will you be my best friend?"

"Me?"

"Yes, you."

"Well, yes. That would be fine."

He nodded and stayed with Sylvie for sometime. Sylvie liked him, I

could tell. Her tail swished quite
happily as he caressed her forehead.
"I'm rather happy now. I think I'll
get going now. I'm going to be
needing to see you again before I go
back to Oxford."

"I think that would be good."

Ronan got up and took his jacket.
There was a certain pause that neither
of us wanted to break into a
conversation. I wasn't sure what he
was to me. A friend, surely. Someone
who came when I was going through a
difficult patch at work.

"Will you be working with
Dorian?" I hated mentioning her name.

"No, I'll be doing some research
and taking my laptop with me to do
outside work. I'm not sure I will

like being in the laboratory today.
Dorian's trying to make it so we are
collaborating. She's not a
collaborator to my mind. I think
Crelon's a fake. I'll have to tell
Sydnor my opinion."

"That's a revelation."

"You know it's true, don't you?"

"But you were the one who showed
it to me."

"Not all. I think you were just
hanging out with them and now you're
free of them. Be happy. I'll have to
extricate myself in my own way."

He had a look on his face that
made her feel sad for him. "Will you
be alright?"

"I will."

"Good."

He smiled at me in a dismissive
manner, but still with a kindly look.
"Sylvie will be needing to have your
company now. Enjoy your first day at
the bakery."

"I will."

"If I need to talk to you I will
send you a text, shall I?"

We took out our cell phones and
exchanged numbers. "Ok good." Ronan
said finally, pocketing the cell and
then heading to the door. He looked at
it and seemed to have a concerned
look. "You have lived here for how
long?"

"Ten years."

"I see. You need a lot more dead
bolt locks."

"I was thinking I'd install

those."

"No need, I'll come tomorrow and put them in."

I felt a swell of gratitude in my chest. "You are so very good." I said with a smile, my hands clasped in front of me.

Ronan shrugged. "I'd do this for my own sister."

"Ok, then thank you."

"Expect me around - well, how long do you work for the bakery?"

"I - I think until three pm."

"I'll be here around three thirty."

"Ok."

He reached over and chucked my chin with a fist. Then he left.

Sylvie stared up at me as I approached the table. "He's very nice, isn't he?"

Sylvie mewed.

I was getting ready to go to sleep when the telephone rang in the hallway. I went to answer it. It was Michel.

"Hallo, Agnes! I have to talk to you immediately. Can you talk to me tonight I mean - now?" He sounded agitated.

"Why, Michel, yes. You can talk. What can I do for you?" I stood on my heels, trying to imagine him looking excited and agitated.

"I need you to come back to work

for me." The words came out in a rush. I almost laughed at his agitation and the way he came to the truth of what he wanted to say. I waited for more to come out of his mouth. That was a long wait, and yet before I could say anything, he added: "We realize that you are an important person in the laboratory. We - I mean - I got a call from the big man and he was unhappy that you left-precipitately. He wants to see you tomorrow. In his office. Can you come?"

He was panting at the end of his speech.

"Of course, Michel, I can come tomorrow. Are you asking me to come back to work?"

"Yes, I am. I want you to work
with that Oxford team of men who want
to ask you for directions on the
procedure to isolate these nerve
cells. We want this to be done."

"Why did you want me to leave
Michel?"

"I am not sure." He sounded
grieved. "I had a bad scene with
Dorian. She was demanding and I gave
in. Now the big man is mad at her
too. I will have to talk to her and
make her realize she can't have
everything she wants."

"Good, Michel. I will come back.
But I am not sure that I can work with
Dorian any longer."

"Please, Agnes, for the love of
God, try to get along with Dorian. She

is almost finished with her doctorate.
Once she leaves you can have peace and
quiet and work on your stuff. Will
you tolerate Dorian? For me? For the
group>"

'Ok, Michel. I'll try to hold my
tongue with Dorian. She needs to see
a shrink more than anyone I know."

"Ha."

"I'll see you in the morning
then."

"Ok, good. Thank you, Agnes."

He rang off with a chuckle in his
voice. I was gratified by his
reaction and then I went to my room
and get into the covers. "What a
day!" I sighed with relief.

Chapter Twelve

I awoke with a start. I was
supposed to see Madame Cortes today.
I hurried with my morning routine and
decided to pick up my breakfast and
drop by the Cortes store to tell her
that I had my job back and that I
wouldn't be working in her bakery that
day.

I hastily threw on a long wool
scarf over my black turtlenecks
sweater and long leggings. I told
Sylvie as I left to take care of the
house.

The weather was chilly and it
braced me. I was excited that I was
going back to my job. The cafe was
still dark but there was a light
inside. I tapped on their door.
After a while, Madame Cortes came out
and let me inside.

I hurriedly told her of a chance
in my circumstances. She nodded,
looking disappointed. "I wish I had
some help," but she smiled finally.
"You need to have a good job these
days. Good luck. Don't do anymore
than you need to - but you have to

find some peace with the people there."

I felt glad she understood. "I'm ok with this job." I said. "They were rather confused about me. I'll try to see what I can do about finding you someone to help you."

She laughed at me. "You are too good and generous with your =self. Don't worry. I'll find someone to help. I am actually putting together an *advertissement* for this position. Go ahead, don't be late for your job!" She shooed me to the door.

I left, feeling happier. I strode over to the Metro station and found myself a seat. There were already a crowd of people in the train.

When I got into the laboratory is
early still and not even Renee was
around to greet me with usual dour
greetings. I took off my scarf and
hung it on the wall. I went around
the laboratory and looked at
everything. All were still in place.
I paused as I passed Dorian's desk and
made a face. She was going to be so
surprised to see me.

As it turned out, Dorian was sick
that day. She called the secretary
who came to our laboratory. "She's
sick."

"Oh, you mean Dorian?" I asked,
looking up from my desk.

"Who else?" The secretary Elise
was making a grimace. "She's
terrible. We heard about what

happened and we told the big boss about it. We want you to stay, Agnes. You are a good worker." With that she beat a retreat back to her office.

When I was ready to do my work, the door opened. Renee entered and paused at the threshold. She stared at me. "You?"

"Yes me." I grinned.

"Oh, my God."

"Well, come on in. I am back."

"What will happen when Dorian comes in?"

"You haven't heard? She's ill today."

Renee, clad in a nice Cheltenham coat put it away and settled into her desk. "I'm sure I don't know."

"Don't worry, I won't make you

sad about not sticking up for me, you silly woman,"

"I was scared. Dorian is an evil one."

"I'm sure she is. I don't know whether I want to share lab space with that female."

There was a silence and Renee fussed over her own work. She muttered to herself about preparing some solutions to do her experiment. Then she went to me and said, "I'm sorry, really Agnes. I am a sad woman. I am already close to being retired. I do not wish to be a source of scandal. I think Dorian has made me terrified."

"I'll have to be sure that she doesn't terrify me. But I wanted to leave here. I wish she'd finish up

and get out and work for someone
else."

The door opened and Crelon came
in. He looked at us and his face
betrayed the shame he felt for having
given into Dorian's wishes. "There
you are. Look here, I'm going to have
a meeting with the Oxford team. As
you know, they are interested in
sharing some information with us. I
think you should be with us to talk."

"I'll be here."

"Good. Now, I've told HR to
rescind the paperwork about your
dismissal. We won't talk about it
again, shall we?"

'Fine." I smiled at him somewhat
formally. I still thought he was too
susceptible to the whims of the people

who held sway with him.

I let him leave and Renee and I
went along with our work.

Then I remembered that I had
nothing for breakfast. I had to go and
find something to eat. I said nothing
to Renee but left the lab. It wasn't
for me to offer her something to eat
from the cafeteria. I'd learned by
then that I wasn't going to be
someone's lackey. It made me feel
guilty still, but I had to be more
independent.

I decided to eat at the cafeteria
and ordered my croissant and coffee.
Then I saw that they had soufflé so I
had that too. I realized that my
morning was an early one and I needed
to make up for the chilly walk to the

Metro and the lack of sleep for I had
to wake up to tell Madame Cortes that
I wasn't going to work for her after
all.

When I was halfway through my
meal, I sensed a presence behind me.
I looked up. It was Ronan. He was
smiling down at me and said, "So
you're back!"

"Yes. I am back."   I leaned
back to observe him. He looked quite
nice in his dark coat and slacks. He
had a messenger bag which he dumped on
the chair next to mine. "Join you?"
He asked.

"Of course!"

"I'll get something to eat and
I'll be back." He walked away and
watched him with a smile on my face.

I thought how nice it was to have someone who was so good to see every day. I wanted him to work in the lab everyday so that I would be happier - looking forward to many days of good company.

By the time he got back, I was tackling the soufflé. He had a large breakfast and I watched him eat and he was quiet as he did so.

"Did you know I'd be back?" I asked him, surprised at my words.

"I did not." He said, sipping his coffee. "But I mentioned something to the boss."

"Which boss?"

"Mr. Hardaway."

"Oh HIM," I gasped.

"Yes, him." His eyebrows

wiggled. "I told him that you had been let go." Ronan hesitated. "I told him you were sacked."

"Oh, Ronan, you didn't!" I gasped.

"Yes I did. He hadn't' heard. He looked surprised. I think that got Crelon's rear in a sling, if you pardon the expression."

I laughed and then I stopped laughing.

"Why did you stop? I like to hear you laugh."

"Well, I got nervous."

"Why?"

"What if someone heard you?"

"No. Nobody's around."

I ate my soufflé with more relish. "I'm sure that Crelon was frantic. He called me last night and begged me to come back."

"Good. That's what I wanted."

I marveled at him. "You did this, Ronan!"

"I did not do much. I wanted to keep you in this lab. You're very smart. I understand that you'd probably be happier working in a bakery. But," He raised his hand. "You have a lot of knowledge that our group needs."

"More than Dorian's?" I lifted a skeptical eyebrow.

"More than Dorian's," Ronan said with a knowing smile.

"Oh, Ronan."

"I know I'm a meddler."

"No you're a Godsend."

He laughed. "Haha. I'm a Godsend she says."

"Well, I'm sure there'll be a lot of talk."

"No. Maybe."

"I'd better get back upstairs. You don't mind if I left you?"

"No, I don't. Best not to talk about us seeing each other here. I'll pretend I'm as surprised to see you."

He winked.

I got up and took my tray to the trolley and left. My heart was soaring and I felt so giddy. Ronan was such a nice man, I told myself.

I was still walking on clouds when I got off the elevator and ran into Dorian. I thought she'd called in sick but she was there in person.

She saw me and then walked the other way.

I said nothing but proceeded to my laboratory. She seemed to have been told from the way she avoided speaking to me. I got to the lab and noticed that her desk was cleared of her stuff. Renee looked as though she wanted to avoid any conversation.

I decided not to mention the cleared desk. Obviously Dorian found it difficult to work in the same room as me.

Finally, Renée relented and said, "Dorian's been assigned to Room Three. She said she has most of her lab stuff there. Crelon said it was ok."

"Good." I said with a nod. I marched to my desk and settled down, feeling as though the day was going well. "I was told she was sick today."

Renee sniffed. "She was well enough to change labs."

I shrugged, I couldn't care less.

The rest of the day went well. I went to conference with Crelon, Hardaway and Ronan and his supervisor Sydnor. I felt rather special, being the only woman in the group.

Crelon started things by saying, "Agnes here has the technique we need for your project to continue without fail. She needs to make this clear in a brief article with the procedure for you. Now," he glanced at Ronan, "Ronan, you might be the point man to get this article, am I right?"

"Yes, well," Sydnor interrupted. "I'd like to have a copy as well."

"Yes, of course." Crelon said, with a slight smile. He looked at Ronan who had an expressionless face.

"I'll be talking to Agnes at length about it, if I may." Ronan said.

"Oh yes that would be good." Crelon bent a stare at Agnes. "You do have time to talk to each other, I'm assuming. Your experiment on the nerve cells is almost finished, am I right?"

"Yes, it is almost finished." I said in reply. "But if Ronan wishes to see this as well it dovetails into the article I'm to write."

"That would work well." Ronan
said coolly.

"I think that's should do it."
Sydnor said, folding his agenda book
that sat in front of him on the table.
It signaled the end of the discussion.

There was a general murmur. I
rose and everyone else did. Ronan
stood back and let everyone else
leave. Once we were alone, he turned
to me with a serious look in his eyes.
"I'm grateful for your generosity with
your procedure. I'll be looking
forward to read your article."

"It shouldn't take long."

"Take your time. Any details
would be helpful."

Ronan went to the door. Then he
paused. "I'm wondering whether you

might wish to visit Oxford and
supervise this procedure?"

I stood rooted to the ground,
feeling somewhat shocked. Oxford. The
very name meant such a great deal to
everyone who knew about science.

"Why, Ronan," I almost gasped
the response. "I'd be honored to come
to Oxford to visit."

"We can arrange that." Ronan
said coolly again. He left and I
followed slowly and went as though in
a trance to my laboratory.

Renee looked up from her desk and
saw me. "Good meeting?"

'Yes, it was."

"Good. I'm glad." Renee said
with a conclusive tone in her voice.

"I think things are going to be

ok." I said to myself. But a certain thought hovered over my head and told me that it wasn't really going to be ok.

Later as I was going into my laboratory experiments I kept thinking of the exchange in the meeting I had with Crelon and the group. I also felt as though I had a thought of Dorian who was the furthest in my mind since she left the laboratory we worked in for the last few years together but separately. I wondered what she was doing but I shook my head. Her work was nothing to do with mine. Her ideas weren't mine. It was a problem getting rid of her having left - in my mind, at least. Why did

I care what she was doing now? It
bothered me and I decided to take a
walk as a break, refreshing my mind.

I stepped out of the building. I
had my shawl around me and I decided
to go to one of the nearby stores and
buy a packet of cigarettes. I hadn't
smoked in a while but today I decided
to take up smoking again.

I took the first drag of smoke
from the cigarette and I immediately
felt a loosening of the constraints
that I felt from the time I left the
meeting. I saw a thought of Dorian
somewhere floating away. I walked
some more, until I arrived at the
bridge, Pont Neuf, where I was a few
days ago. I had mourned the loss of

Paul, but now I felt free of him. I
was over him for real. I didn't miss
him. No mention of anything that had
to do with him, his Englishness, nor
his interest in someone else who was
more glamorous than me, had made me
feel any pangs of regret.

I wondered whether I should tell
Dr. Prince about it. I will see him in
a few days, I knew.

Somewhere from where I stood, I
saw a familiar figure walking towards
me. It was Ronan. He didn't see me
from where I was. It was beginning to
cloud over, and the sun was waning.

I decided to return to the lab.
I finished my cigarette and threw it
away. I regretted that act. Paris was
a beautiful city. I shouldn't have

tossed the spent cigarette but now it was floating on the Seine and it would be churned up by one of the floating barges that crossed it to parts unknown.

"Agnes!"

I heard Ronan's voice.

I turned. He was almost upon me. His cheeks were red, from having been outdoors for a while. Longer than while I was outside.

"Hi Ronan."

"What are you doing outside?"

I could have asked him the same question.

"I like to walk when there's too much stress in my system. I had a good meeting with you today. Too many thoughts crowded my mind," I replied, smiling up at him.

He nodded. "It's rather crisp out. You're not wearing a coat."

"I do ok with this on."

"You're a brave girl. It's almost November."

"I think you could do with a coat yourself," I noted his jacket and nothing else over it.

He shrugged as he surveyed himself from his vantage point. "I walk like this in Oxford - bracing the mind."

"I agree."

"What do you say you and I head back to Oxford?"

The question was surprising. "Did you mean I go to Oxford with you?"

"Yes, why not. I'll have all I need in the laboratory. You and I can go through your procedure and get some experiments done."

"Is that something I can do? I need to get permission."

'Are you up to it? That's the more important question."

"Where will I stay? Do they have housing?"

"Yes."

"What about - oh my cat Sylvie." I worried aloud.

"Bring her along." Ronan waved his hand expansively.

"Oh my God." I laughed. We took a walk back to the laboratory.

"You don't need to stay long. I can get things set up. We'll work on a couple of runs of the experiment."

"You can ask. Tell them it's ok
with me." I felt a shiver of
excitement. "I've never gone to any
place to work on an experiment."

He had a big grin on his face.
"I'll be so excited. Oer the moon
about it. You and I will be a great
duo."

We laughed as we got on our way
back to the lab.

Chapter Thirteen

We decided to stop by the
cafeteria and have a cup of coffee
before heading back to the laboratory.
However, when we were on our way to
the lab, a team of emergency
technicians trooped by us and held up
the elevators. People scratched their

heads and wondered aloud what was happening.

Someone mentioned that there was a sick person in Hardaway's lab.

Ronan and I stared at each other in disbelief. "Who would it be who was sick?" I asked him.

"Let's wait and see who they take out of there."

We stood around and sipped our coffee. We couldn't discuss any plans because it was a public location we were in. The elevators were humming as always. But people were barred from going in and out. The gendarme from the emergency unit held the elevators under his control.

"What happened, *gendarme?*" Asked someone near us.

"I do not know, rightly." He coughed. "Not something we can discuss, *Mam'sel*,"

"Let's go back and finish this coffee," suggested Ronan. "I'm sure that we can't do anything at this time."

"What if it's Renee?"

"So what if it's Renee?" He coolly asked, steering me back into the cafeteria's premises. "She's not prone to having a heart attack or fainting is she?"

'No, but - "

"Speculations won't help."'

"I have an iPhone. What if I called?"

"I wouldn't call. They would be

sad and frazzled. Just relax.
Whatever happened they have it under
control."

'Ok, you are the boss," I
grinned at him.

"Just for that I will buy you a
pastry," Ronan said and grinned back
at me.

We talked at length about
everything that I did in the lab. He
wasn't taking notes but he kept saying
"Mm" and seemed to file everything I
told him in his mind, "I am going to
ask Crelon if he can spare you a few
weeks' time, to work with us in
Oxford," Ronan said again,'

"Oh, that would be lovely," I

said, feeling special,'

"I would be grateful for your company in the lab."

He seemed to be serious in stating this. I looked away and tried not to read too much into it. I had been there before when Paul would say something similar to me. I wasn't going to be hooked into another love affair. LOVE, the words flashed in my mind. NO, I wasn't in love again. I tried not to look a Ronan. I couldn't believe how fast my mind sped. No, I wasn't in love. This man was a good sort, and he was decent to me. No, I'm not in love with him, I surely am not, said I to myself.

It bothered me, nonetheless. My heart was fluttering without much reason unless - unless he was really making me feel as though I were falling in love with him. It was too soon, I thought, no it was too soon.

We didn't speak for a few minutes. Then there was a slight commotion and the door to the cafe opened and behind the door rushed the emergency technicians and their stretcher which bore a person who was enshrouded in a sheet. We couldn't tell who it was. The person's face was covered with an oxygen mask and from this distance we weren't sure if it was a man or a woman. But, Michel was walking alongside, and then he looked into the cafeteria and saw us. He waved the technicians goodbye and hurried into the cafeteria.

"Thank God you're here, Agnes. Ronan." He said in a rush, wiping his face as it was streaming with sweat. "Something bad has happened."

"What happened?: We both asked together. I added, "They said it was in the Laboratory."

"It's Dorian."

'Dorian?" I asked, blankly.

"Dorian's sick. She was found hyperventilating in the fourth lab. She's terribly ill. I don't know if she'll make it," Michel said, staring unseeingly at the departing emergency personnel.

"Does she have any relatives that you can contact.?" Asked Ronan.

"No, she has a boyfriend, but he's out of town all the time,"

Crelon replied'

"What happened? Did she just
faint away or what?" I asked.

"She was found wheezing in the
tissue culture laboratory, and when
someone asked her what she was
feeling, Dorian tried to get up from
her chair and fainted dead away,"
Crelon shrugged. "They called the
hospital. And here they are taking her
away."

"Did they have any preliminary
diagnosis?" Asked Ronan.

"No - well - I think they said
she night have had a heart attack,"

'Oh my God". I gasped. "She's so
young. And she seems to be healthy,"

"Yes she does doesn't she?"
Ronan agreed.'

"Well, this is too much." Crelon complained. "I'm not happy at all... If she survives she might have a long convalescence. And her degree should be conveyed soon. Her presentation for orals will be soon along. I don't know. I don't like how she's been in high dudgeon."

"She's always in a state," I commented.

Ronan and Crelon looked at me. "What do you mean?" Asked Crelon.

"All I mean is that she's always upset about something or other."

"And she was the one who wanted Agnes to be let go wasn't it her?: Ronan asked.

Crelon looked sheepishly at him. "That is no longer the issue. I've

had a talk with Dorian. She will be
told what to expect. I think she
might have been suffering from a great
disappointment,"

"I think she needs to take a
vacation". I said,'

The conversation was becoming
uncomfortable for me. It seemed as
though what happened with me and
Dorian night have precipitated her
collapse. But it wasn't that bad, I
thought. But I knew Dorian was never
going to be the same in her attitude
towards me, for Crelon changed his
mind, and Hardaway backed me and so
did other personnel who wanted me to
stay. That might have made Dorian
feel completely surrounded and that
was what happened to cause her to

collapse.

Ronan broke our reverie. "Well, I'm needing to go up and take Agnes to the conference room. If you'll excuse us, Crelon," he said coolly, smiling somewhat offhandedly,

"Of course, we should start talking about the experiments that you will need to work one shall we?"

"Yes, I'd like to propose that Agnes join us in Oxford in a few days' time. I want her to set up the laboratory with everything that we will need to duplicate the procedures we need for this research to come along," Ronan said breezily,'

"Oh my," Crelon looked surprised. "If that's the case I suppose I can spare Agnes for a few days."

"I think we can keep her for a
few weeks - a month or so?"

"I - I - I - "

"Let's talk about it later shall
e=we?"

Ok let's do that," Crelon said
with a slight smile. He looked at me
with dawning respect. "Agnes, you
will need to make arrangements - "

For what>? I asked in my head.
"I'll leave it to Ronan and well,
Oxford to figure out how they need me
to help them,"

"I'll have to ask Hardaway for
permission." Ronan said.

"That would be the one to ask,"
Crelon said with a failing accent.
"I'm surely not the one to ask. I do
not know whether I should go after

Dorian."

"I should go and find out,"
Ronan said helpfully.

With that, Crelon left us
standing.

I returned with Ronan to the Lab
and found the place in a state of
unsettledness. People were huddled in
groups. The doors of the labs were
open. The workers hurried off to
disappear as soon as they saw us.
Ronan and I looked at each other in
wonderment.

I went to a coworker, Denise, who
was cleaning up where Dorian's lab was
located. "What's happened?'

Denise shrugged. "Someone called
the alarm. They found Dorian gasping

for air. I thought she was on drugs,
myself."

"Drugs?" I echoed.

"Yes, did not you know? She is a
user of drugs. She tried to hide it
but some of us found her smoking
something. We told her it was
prohibited." Denise shook her head.
"I think she's going to die. They
tried to help, the emergency people."

"Ronan, that's incredible." I
told him.

"Some people hide it well, but
apparently there were witnesses," he
opined.

We tried to digest this news.
"She was conscious, though, wasn't
she, when they took her away?" I
asked Denise, who looked reluctant to

converse further.

"I don't know." She left us in a hurry. She muttered to herself, but I didn't catch it.

Ronan took my elbow. "Let's forget about this. We need to find Hardaway's PA and ask her to find us time to talk to him about our plans to go to Oxford together."

I nodded, numbed by what happened. I wasn't fond of Dorian, but she never seemed to exhibit the signs of being a drug addict.

I followed Ronan to Hardaway's office. It was empty of people. It was useless to do business that afternoon. I turned to Ronan. "Why don't I send an email to Elise and ask her to make an appointment for both us?"

"Good idea," Ronan looked bored.
"I'll find Sydnor and tell him what
I'd like to do. Then let's regroup
later or tomorrow morning shall we?"

We smiled at each other and I
felt reassured. This incident with
Dorian was receding from my memory. I
did not like the woman but this was a
definite negative event that anyone
there was ready to forget.

Chapter Fourteen

Dorian was in hospital for the weekend and on Monday morning, Hardaway and Crelon called everyone to the conference room. We weren't given fair warning of a meeting so I felt a certain foreboding that something wasn't gong well. I feared that she died and Hardaway's first words confirmed it.

"We've got news that Dorian has passed away." Hs bushy wh8te brows were furrowed over his long nose.

There was a slight murmur in the ranks. I glanced at Rona who was sitting in the back with his Oxford mates. His face was indecipherable. Renee who sat next to me stifled a shocked epithet.

"What was it that killed her?" Asked William, who wasn't looking too concerned, as he barely spoke to anyone, It seemed to me his interest was misplaced,'

"She had an overdose," Crelon said, "Its not clear but she had methamphetamine in her bloodstream. The woman asphyxiated and she couldn't come out of the coma it gave her. The doctors tried their best.:""

"Parents been told?" The other
technician who was working in Dorian's
lab asked.

"Yes of course, they were with
her at the time she died," replied
Crelon.

"There's been any word on funeral
arrangements?" I had to ask just to
sound concerned. I didn't like Dorian
and her drug use was a news flash to
me.

"I have not heard," replied
Hardaway, giving me a look of
thoughtfulness, "I'm sure we'll hear
about it."

"Right," Crelon said coolly.
"We need to find a way to continue her
research."

"That's for her doctorate, it's going to be a bit tough to get anyone else to do this." Spoke Renee, who wasn't interested in getting snared into doing Dorian's work which never really was much to her concern.

"I think we can hire someone." Hardaway said coldly. "WE are all in this research together. We can try to divvy up the responsibilities.:"

"Not sure I can spare the time," Spoke another fellow who was working in his own field of research. "Dorian's the only one who did work with stuff that had to do with protein purification That stuff is something that takes a lot of time to work on - and learn," He sniffed. His name was Lawrence. He and I never worked together and he wasn't that interested in chumming up with everyone. He wasn't a generous sort. Btu that was how scientific people were in our lab. "I mean to say, she kept her research a big secret and only gave reports sporadically,"

Crelon Looked at him with a glint in this eye. "I know she wasn't good about doing the right thing about sharing."

"This doesn't excuse her behavior about that. We'll have to find a new technician to do this, or recruit a student who's interested in furthering her work," Hardaway said with a doubtful tone.'\

"I'd say we can look at her work and see if it's worth finishing up."

"No PhD going to be given out for
finishing it out," spoke up Renee,
who had echoed my own thoughts.

"I'm sad we're not more
sympathetic." Crelon said. "Never
mind. I'll look at what she's done so
far and I'll make a decision whether
or not to further it or publish as it
stands."

"Sounds fair," Ronan said
finally.

"Thank you Rohan," said Crelon,
smiling at him gratefully.

"Well, is that all?" Lawrence
asked with crispness in his voice.'

"Well, yes." Hardaway and Crelon
looked at each other.'

"Wait," Renee finally raised her
hand. "We never knew she was a drug

addict. What a surprise and she worked in our lab for most of her career here."

"I think this is a well kept secret," I said finally as well. "I'm not a chum of hers but she always carried on without much of any symptoms that she was into this." I realized Dorian would suffer skin problems and that was a methamphetamine symptom, from what I read in literature.

"Well, we all each have to reach out to each other whenever we feel sad." Crelon wiped his lips with a handkerchief he had in his pocket. "We'll have to pass around some sort of hat to help with things won't we, Mr. Hardaway?"

"Whatever you like."

"Well," Sydnor said. "We're
rather sad to hear about it. Our
Group didn't have many plans with
Dorian but she was quite interested in
what we were doing. WE did ask her
about her work, but she was brief
about it."

"That's because - " Someone else
said in the back. We all looked at the
person and it was Lydia Wu, the
Chinese girl who was the part time
worker who made up solutions for
everybody. "Sorry, but she really was
awful to me but she also tried to pass
on her work to anyone who could
because she'd go off for hours to God
knows where."

There was a shocked silence.

Then Crelon coughed. "Let's try to think of her well, being dead."

There was a chuckle but I couldn't tell who did that. I felt sad and amused at the same time. Dorian's life was a puzzle and nobody cared for her and now we had to finally realize how quite tawdry her life was. A glamorous woman who dressed well and did stupid things and asked people to carry on for her while she was off swanning around with her distant lover. I decided not to comment. Piling on bad deeds on a newly dead person wasn't the thing to do, in my opinion.

WE all dispersed and I went with Renee to our lab. Renee had no real words to comment about the meeting but

when we were into our own work, she
said suddenly, "I saw her one time at
a rather strange area in Paris, where
I was stranded one day. It was unlike
her to be there. But she was with a
group of young people and they were
very cheery together," she said in a
reflective tone.

"Well, why were you stranded
there?"

"The Metro was stalled and we all
had to file out and find another place
to get transport home," Renee
replied.

"So she might have been with the
same sort as she I presume."

"Yes." Renee shivered and felt
for her arms with her hands. "I'm
scared to death for some reason."

"Oh bosh." I said. "Whatever for?"

"I don't know."

"I think the police will be around asking questions, Agnes," she predicted.

"Oh God, I hope not. I'll be totally clueless."

"I don't think this will be good for the lab. News travels and then there'll be a story in the papers and her face being so attractive - "

"Oh and are her people rich or something?"

"I think they're moneyed," she replied. "What a mess."

"Don't worry about it." I said with alacrity. "It'll blow over and we'll be finally out of this horrid little death we've had in the lab,"

"I don't like it." Renee sounded
convinced of something,'

I turned around to look at her,
"Do you know something more Renee?" I
asked, then I felt a pang of panic.
If she knew something and she was
going to be asked this would place us
in a sad position in the eyes of the
public. Our laboratory was always
highly respected.

"No, I don't. Just that one
time."

I couldn't resist asking, "Did
you see her with any of these people
later on?"

Renee shook her head.

Chapter Fifteen

The day after Dorian's death, a
man who wore a trench coat came to the
laboratory. He went straight to the
office of Doctor Hardaway. I couldn't
help but notice him. He wore a hat
and looked inscrutable. I was on my
way out of the lab I shared with Renee
and almost bumped into him. He held

up his hand as if to steady me. A
brief nod and then he went on his way.
I watched as he entered the office
which was open as the door was ajar.
I heard him say, "I'm Inspector
Moreau, I've come to speak to your
Superior." He reached into his pocket
and showed her something. The look on
Elise made me feel worried.

Elise murmured something and then
rose from her desk. He followed her
into Hardaway's office.

I went on my way to the common
room where we kept our chemicals and
other solutions for our work and tried
not to think about it. But thoughts
swirled through my mind about the
visit from the Surete.

Later, while Renee and I were

working quietly, the door opened. It
was Doctor Hardaway. He seemed to be
in a sober mood. Behind him walked
Inspector Moreau.

"Renee and Agnes, I'm asked to
tell you that we have the Surete
visiting us," he said without much
ado. "He wants to talk to anyone who
knew Dorian. I'll leave him to you
and then you can go on with your
work."

A clatter sounded as Renee
dropped a pipette on the floor. She
murmured "I'm sorry clumsy of me."

Inspector Moreau looked at Renee
with some suspicion but kept his face
expressionless.

"I'll be seeing you both,
ladies," Hardaway said before he left

us with the Inspector,

"I'm Inspector Moreau,"
reiterated the man. He was not a tall
man but his presence filled me with
dread. I was nervous in the company
of the police. They were always so
serious and, to the point, being
questioned about Dorian filled me with
dread.

He looked at each of us
alternately and then went to talk to
me. "You are?"

"Agnes Dumont, Inspector," I
replied.

"I see. And what do you do
here?"

"I'm a laboratory technician."

"And how long have you worked
here?"

'Three years,"

"Before that where did you work?"

"I was a student - at the Sorbonne," I said lifting my chin.

"And what about Miss Dorian X? Do you know here well?"

"She was a coworker, nothing more," I replied.'

"She worked in this laboratory? Is that not true?" He took out a notepad and scribbled on it.

"She did but she changed labs recently."

Renee who was listening in the background murmured, "Can I go to fetch a chemical from the common room?"

"No you may not," Inspector Moreau said curtly. He turned back to

me. Renee slumped in her chair. "Go
on what made her move?"

"We had a disagreement and she
made my superior fire me. Then when I
was out of my job I went home and
tried to find another job near my
home," I replied.

"Why would she want you fired?
Are you a bad worker?"

"No, sir, I'm a good worker."

"And she was merely trying to
make trouble for you?"

"She didn't like me. She wanted
me to do her work for her. I am not
her maid."

"Ah, so she was some sort of a -
a - " he searched for the right word,
"Bully?"

"I do not think she was that bad

but we didn't get along." I felt a
shiver in my body because I was
telling the truth. Yet somehow in my
mind I was getting myself into more
trouble. Why did I have to tell him
about this firing? I asked myself.

"Ok what about the day she
collapsed. Where were you then?"

"I was downstairs having a coffee
with one of the visiting scientists."

At that point I felt relief.

"Ah I see. Who was this visiting
scientist?

"Dr. Michael Andrews. He's from
Oxford University. They have a group
here to talk to us about our work."

"Ok, that is all. I might want
to see you again. Will you be alright
with that?"

"I am."

He turned away from me and headed for Renee.

I tried to say something but I decided not to add to any more conversations with him.

I saw Renee looked very nervous when he approached her. It almost seemed as though she wanted to shield herself with her arm when he came to her. "What is your name, Madam?"

"Renee Beauvoir," she replied in a small voice.

"What do you do here?"

"I'm another of the technicians here, I work for *M. Le Docteur* Crelon," she replied.

"What about this woman Dorian,

how did you get along with her?"

Renee shrugged. "She was not of my generation. She liked things that I didn't in fashion. But she left me to my own and did her work apart from me."

"So did she respect you?"

"I think she did. She didn't ask me to do her dirty work for her, like she did Agnes." Renee motioned at me with her head inclined.

"Did you notice anything about her behavior on the day she collapsed?"

"No, we were working in separate labs, how could I know?" This time Renee seemed more confident with her answers.

"So is she someone who likes to

be fashionable? Eh?"

He seemed to ask this of both of us because he looked at me and her alternately.

"She's fashionable enough, but we have the different fashions we like," Renee said.

"She has a way with clothes that's true," I replied.

"Is this fashion thing a big deal with her? Did she for example wear very expensive clothes to work?"

Renee laughed as though he was saying something that seemed ridiculous. "I'm not sure. She never bragged about her clothing. Nor did she say she received a big fashion outfit from her boyfriend," her voice was still mirthful.

"Ah, boyfriend," *M'sieur* Inspector said. "What about the boyfriend. Who was this man?"

"He was from out of town. He had a funny named, like Roalph Something or other," I replied.

"Why did he live out of town?"

"I don't know, but she pleaded many times to have us help her work while she went off to see him out f town." I replied with a small moue. "I don't know anything more about him."

"Did they plan to marry soon?"

Renee shook her head, "No, she never talked about marriage. She's one of those women who have affairs but never get married."

He looked disgusted at this.

Then he snapped his little notebook
shut. "I'll have to ask - do you at
all remember this Roalph's last
name?":

'No," Renee and I said together.

"Well, that will have to do. I
still don't know how to reach her
parents."

"Her parents live very far from
here- somewhere like in Marseille,"
Renee volunteered.

He nodded. "That's what I hear
from Doctor Hardaway," he said with a
small grunt. "I think we might be
finished."

Renee said something but then she
didn't go on. The inspector didn't
seem to hear her. He walked to the
door and then he shut it behind him.

I tried not to say much to Renee but I remembered that she told me that she saw Dorian with a few unsavory people around the Metro area. I wondered what to do. Then I realized it wasn't me who had to say it but Renee. Yet, something about my silence bothered me.

I went out of the lab and walked aimlessly as though in search of something else to think about. Just then Michael came out of his lab and saw me. He smiled at me with great relief,' Ah, there you are what have you been up to, Agnes?"

"Oh the police came to ask questions about Dorian," I said with a sigh. I was grateful I had him to tell this piece of news.

"I'm sorry. Was it an ordeal?"
He asked me.

"Well, I am nervous when it comes
to the police. They are always so
officious and make you think that you
did something wrong."

"Oh, I see." A slight frown
crossed his face. "I don't know why
you'd be that nervous around them,
Agnes."

"They make me nervous, that is
about it." I said with more emphasis.
"I'm still a bit bothered by
something. I wonder if I could tell
you what it is. - You seem to be more
level headed than everyone else here
today."

"If that's all then I'm all
ears." He took me aside to a small

alcove. "What is it that you are troubled about?"

I told him about what Renee said to me about seeing Dorian in an unsavory part of the Metro. He listened impassively. Then he said, "And she didn't tell the policeman?"

"No, she didn't." I said realizing something and added, "But he never really asked the question about her friends - Dorian's I mean."

"Oh ok, so it never touched that subject did it?" He looked almost angry. "Well, what sort of policemen is that that doesn't ask questions about the victim's friends?"

"He asked about Dorian's boyfriend and her family. But that was all."

"Ok, don't worry too much. I'm sure he's doing preliminary work and he could come back."

I sighed again and then smiled finally. "I think that will be ok. I can stand seeing him again. I didn't do anything about her problems,"

'No," Ronan stared down at me and said it again, "No."

I looked up at him and wondered why he looked so formal. "I think I'd better go to the laboratory library now. I need to look up an article that might help my work."

He nodded and let me go.

Chapter Sixteen

I worked on my project in the
library of the X Institute in relative
silence. But there were some voices
that bothered me. I wondered who they
were. I looked up and regarded the
window in front of me which gave a
lovely view of the Eiffel Tower in a
misty atmosphere. Snow flakes were

coming down. It was a beautiful view. I wish that I could get my cell phone to take a picture of the view.

As I did, the voices came to rise where I could understand what they were saying.

"No, I do NOT want anyone to know about Dorian!"

I was shocked. It was Renee who was saying this to someone who's voice I wasn't able to discern completely.

Renee's voice seemed to be terrified. "She was a good person to me. I have no money but what I get from this job. She gave me a lot of money so I can go shopping and have lovely food."

The other voice said something and its made Renee sad and she sobbed,

"I don't want to give evidence. I
can't tell anything. Don't bother me
anymore!"

There was a sound of feet running
away and then the bang of a distant
door.

I looked around and wondered
whether I ought to go out of the
library and see who it was who got
Renee nervous. I left my seat and
walked quickly to the door and looked
out.

The only person I saw was Michel
Crelon who was walking out of the room
next door. I realized that the room
next door was where the conversation
was held. There was not a sign of
Renee anywhere.

I went back to my seat and pored

over the big volume of the Journal of
Neurology and tried to forget about
what I heard. If Renee and Michel
were arguing then it was going to be a
scandal if they knew what was going on
with Dorian and how she died.

I tried to forget the
conversation. But as I took notes
from the Journal of Neurology, the
words came back to mind. So, Dorian
gave Renee money. For what reason?
And why did she not wish to give
evidence? What did she know about
Dorian and her death that she had to
give evidence? And, more importantly,
why was it Michel Crelon who talked to
her about Dorian this way?

I paused in my note taking and
chewed on the end of the pen, thinking

again. I realized I have found myself
in the middle of a murder mystery. Or
did I get hasty about this? Was
Dorian murdered? The idea made me feel
slight shiver in my bones. It was
something to think about. Why would
Dorian get murdered? Why does Crelon
know about this? Did that Inspector
talk to him? Oh, my God, I told
myself, what are we going to be
facing? I did not want to know. I
wanted to fly away out of this
seemingly peaceful existence in the
Laboratory H that made me have a
comfortable existence and live in a
beautiful City of Paris where I could
have all the baguettes in the world.

I hated to think any further. I
sat back and looked longingly at the

large book in front of me. I wanted
to keep taking notes. Then, I
realized, I could easily have used the
copy machine to take the article and
keep it in my binder. I sighed and
wished that this solution would remove
the growing fear in m y heart and give
me back my placid existence. Me,
Agnes Dumont, a mere technician in a
large laboratory. Someone who had a
normal family. Someone who went to
school ad graduated with good marks.
Now, having heard this.

Then I wondered whether this
conversation was real or made to have
someone like me start thinking
wildly. Did Crelon have a grudge
against me? Did he know that I was in
this room?

I shook my head with sadness.

That was when Andrew came into the library and caught me looking pitiful. He didn't seem to notice at first. "Oh, hi," he said. "I'm sure I left something here."

"Hi," I said back, trying to look more professional, with my pen finally finding itself against the notepaper I had on the desk. "I've not seen anything here that could be out of place."

"Oh, it's my lab notebook."

"Oh."

"I wondered whether now that I've found you," Ronan said as he came to my side. "Would you like to have a light lunch at the bistro next to the laboratory? It's called *Le Bistor*

Ariel."

I hadn't remembered a bistro like this but that was because I never looked for a place nearby for a lunch hour. I always took my lunch at my desk.

"I'd love to go," I said finally.

"Good." He glanced at his watch. "Let's go now. I'm famished. I'll order a huge meal. The French like to serve small servings, I've noticed. I might order a five course meal."

I laughed at him, finally the shreds of fear had left my shoulders. "I would like to have a five course meal myself, but I cannot afford it."

"No fear, my dear Agnes," Ronan smiled. "I'll buy your lunch."

"Oh my God, would you?"

"Yes, of course!" He took my
hand and I left everything except my
notebook and pen. Ronan noticed them
and said, "Why don't you drop them off
at your lab and meet me at the
elevators?"

I nodded, and separated from him
outside the library and went off to my
laboratory where it was empty of
people. I realized that Renee's
presence would be a problem for me
now. She was nowhere to be seen.

I took my coat and purse and
rushed out the door, and fairly ran to
the elevators and saw Ronan loitering
about, his face a bit of a study.

"Here I am," I said.

"Good, let's go," said Ronan,

taking me into the elevator and
letting the door close in front of us.

Le Bistro Ariel was a cosy place,
something that reminded me of a warm
hall where diners had the privacy that
other eating places lacked. At the
end of the hall was a huge fireplace
that occupied the entire wall, and a
huge flame licked at the sides of the
fireplace, leaping up from its origin
where dark wood logs were piled at the
bottom.

The waiter came to take us to our
table which was not far from the
fireplace, which was so very
satisfying to me. "Ohhh, this feels
very good, Ronan!" I exclaimed.

"It does, doesn't it?"

"Would you like something for a drink?" Asked the waiter.

"A bottle of your best Burgundy". Replied Ronan.

The waiter nodded approvingly and left us.

"I really like this place Michael. I've lived and worked here in Paris for such a long time and I've not discovered it," I commented. I sat half reclining, feeling the stress flow out of my body.

"You look peaked, my girl," Ronan observed.

"I've been working in the library," I replied, as though it would suffice as reason enough for me looking peaked.

"I'm thinking it's more than

that," Ronan said. "Is it something
to do with Dorian's death?"

"I think you've hit on it," I
nodded, sighing. I sat up and leaned
forward to talk more confidentially.
"I've overheard something, a short
conversation between Renee and
Michel."

"What was it about?"

"I heard something that sounded
as though Renee knew about Dorian's
death. Or had information and she
wouldn't do it."

"I see," Ronan said, but he said
nothing more as the waiter appeared
with our wine and the glasses.

"Would you like to know what our
day's special is?" Asked the waiter.

We nodded. Whereupon the waiter

gave us a concise description of what
our meal would be like if we ordered
it. Ronan approved it promptly and
then we were alone again, Ronan
looked sideways before he talked to
me, "Tell me more about this
conversation"

"I'm not sure what it was really.
But it was Renee's voice I heard for
sure. Michel's voice was muffled. I
couldn't make out his words but Renee
said she wouldn't come forward to say
what she knew about Dorian"

"Do you have any inkling what she
might know about Dorian?"

Ronan's eyes were focused on me
with such an intensity that I was
breathless.

"Well, I have to admit she said

something to me one time when Dorian
just died."

"What was it?"

"I'm not totally sure about this
but she mentioned that she saw Dorian
somewhere in a bad neighborhood along
the Metro line. I asked her why would
she see Dorian there at such a time,
but she replied that the Metro had
broken down and the train had to let
the passengers alight. Everyone went
home on foot that night."

"Oh, and this is where she might
have walked past Dorian who was doing
what?"

I hesitated. "Well, nothing
really. But Dorian was with people who
looked suspicious. Bad sorts."

"Oh," Ronan leaned back as the

waiter came to start serving us with
hot beefy soup and a baguette. After
the waiter left, Ronan continued to
ask, "So she was with bad sorts.
Nothing tells me this is extraordinary
unless you do not know Dorian very
well."

"No I do not know her, did not
know here very well. She was not my
type of friend. I did not like her.
We did not like each other. You know
she wanted me to be fired. She's that
sort of woman. Cruel and vindictive.
And lazy. She lets others do her job
and then she gets the applause."

"And did she not have friends
come by to say hello who were
presentable enough?"

"No, she kept her private life to

herself."

"But Renee seemed to know what she was really into? Drugs and all that?"

"Well, since we discovered Dorian died from an overdose of methamphetamine, it would make sense that she was likely getting this drug from bad sorts does it not?"

"Yes. I agree." Ronan picked up his fork and said "Eat, let's enjoy the food. I'm interested in this Dorian and her double life now."

We ate in silence for a while. Then Ronan said suddenly, "I'm thinking that Dorian was a drug addict and also dealt drugs - why else would she be with unsavory people in a bad neighborhood?"

"Really, you think so?" I looked
at him eagerly. This was matching my
idea of Dorian. "She was always
dressed so well, and I can wager that
she bought expensive clothes from
designers."

"Ah and what car did she drive?"
His eyes were alight with humour.

"I think she drove a Fiat."

"Those aren't cheap."

"I also know she traveled a lot.
Her boyfriend lived outside Paris.
They would see each other every
weekend and sometimes he'd visit her
during the week. That's when she'd ask
somebody to help her with her work
because she couldn't stay to finish
it."

"She sounds like a spoiled brat,"

he commented. "Finish you soup."

"I know I tend to dawdle with my soup," I laughed at him.

"You know I'd like to know more about you, Agnes," he said, his eyes were solemn.

I flushed and felt shy. "What do you want to know about me?"

"You're an attractive girl - why aren't you with someone? Or married with children?"

I tried not to feel the pang of regret. "I was in love before. He went for someone else. That's it."

He looked at me with sympathy. "I am so sorry."

"Yes, it happened seven years ago. I really fell for him. He was a bastard but it seemed as though I could never get over him."

He leaned back and let go of his fork. It dropped on the table. "I'm not happy that he treated you badly. You didn't realize he was this bad?"

"No, I fell for his lies."

"And nobody else has stolen your heart?"

I laughed at him at his words. "You sound like a Frenchman when you say that."

"I'm one-fifth French, does that work?"

We both erupted in laughter. Then he became serious. "You see, I'd like to know you better. I want us to be more than friends."

I felt a sudden thrill that rose from my stomach and reached into my chest. "I'm - I'm - "

"So do you think we can be more than friends?" He interrupted me.

"Well, how can we? You live in England and I live in Paris, here." I tried to be practical.

"No, I don't have to live in England."

"Really?" I couldn't believe my ears.

"Really."

I was about to say something then the waiter came to give us our check. "I'll take care of it," said Ronan. He looked at me with a knowing eye. "Agnes, we need to meet again later tonight. Will you go out with me for a quiet dinner?"

"Oh yes," I said with a smile.

It was a very big smile and I felt happy. This man wanted me. I was so happy. How can a girl say no when this man who was so handsome and very charming wanted to take me out for dinner and start a - dare I say it - a love affair?

Chapter Seventeen

When we came back to work, Renee
was not in her usual station in the
laboratory. I saw her coat was gone
so I surmised she went out to have
lunch. It was not out of the ordinary
in her to have lunch outside the
laboratory. In fact, with the
cafeteria in the first floor, many of

the lab workers went downstairs to
eat. But with Renee's coat gone, I
decided she had a more formal reason
to go for lunch outside of the
building.

I was left at my laboratory by
Michael who smiled at me with a
special squeeze on my arm with his
capable hand before he went back to
his work. "I'll see later," he said.

"Yes," I replied, but felt
unable to add anything else. I didn't
want to break the spell that was
between us. I tried to see if anyone
else was witnessing our leave-taking
after lunch and nobody was around,

I puttered around the laboratory
and decided it was too late to start
an experiment that might run through

past five o'clock this afternoon. So
I made some reagents and felt rather
satisfied that these were ready to use
whenever anyone wanted them.

It was after three o'clock that
Crelon came into the lab. "Renee - I
need Renee," he said peremptorily,
bursting into the room with his usual
gusty attitude.

"I haven't seen her since I came
back from lunch," I replied, looking
up from my desk.

"I can't believe it," he
exclaimed.

"Well, believe it. She didn't
leave me a note either."

"Did she take her coat?"

"Yes, she did," I nodded.

"Well, she might have decided to

take the rest of the day off."

"Good for her don't you think?"

"No, it isn't good for me.
Listen, since you're here," Crelon
decidedly said. "I need to get some of
her results. Could you rummage through
her lab notebook and find the entries
from the last five days of her work?
You can scan them in the copy machine
and give them to me. I'll be in my
office." With that he disappeared
into the hallway.

I felt reluctant to rummage as he
said through Renee's notebook. It
seem too much for me to do, as I
respected Renee's work. I hadn't had
to do that for anyone since I started
with Crespo and Hardaway. But, I
followed Crelon's directions and

looked for Renee's notebook.

Renee was a good laboratory technician and her notebooks were very neatly. Stacked on the top of her desk. I looked for the most recent notebook. It was there right where I would have predicted. I went through it and then took it to the copy machine where I copied several pages of her work. I didn't see anyone on the way to Crelon's office.

Crelon was on the phone when I got there. "I'm looking for those now, ah," Crelon said and then saw me enter his office. "I've got the lab notes. Thank you Agnes."

I said nothing and took the lab notebook back to Renee's desk.

I sat back in my desk and then I

felt rather strange. I went in search
of Ronan and saw him having a cup of
coffee chatting with his colleague.
He saw me and got up to talk to me.

"What's up?"

"Michel asked me for Renee's
notebook."

"Why?"

"Oh, he wanted them?" Ronan
looked around. "Where is Renee
anyway? She's not here?"

"No," I drew closer to him as
though a grasping motion had tried to
come for me from behind. "Oh, Ronan,
this isn't good."

"You're shivering."

"I'm sorry, this isn't me. I
don't know why I'm feeling scared."

"I'm going to take you home now,"

"No, it will be ok. Just knowing you're around will make it better."

He took me in his arms and held me lightly. "I'll be here. Don't worry."

"I'm sorry. This is very strange indeed."

"I'm wondering whether you are taking medication?"

"I have been. I've been seeing a psychiatrist."

"Oh?"

"Yes, after I had a breakup with that horrid Paul, I saw a psychiatrist to get over the breakup."

Ronan rested his chin on my head and smiled. "You see, that might be that you are getting too much of this medication."

"Well, it's a low dose. How could it be doing that?"

He looked puzzled. "I don't know Agnes. I do not know."

As we kept talking the door opened. It was the Surete officer. *"Bon jour. Excusez moi.* Looking for Mrs. Renee Beauvoir's friend, Agnes Dumond."

I started. "That's me."

Ronan stood between me and the officer. "What is the matter?"

"Who are you?" Demanded the officer,

"I'm Agnes good friend - Ronan Michaels."

"Well, we have news about Mrs Beauvoir."

I sensed Ronan steel himself.

"Go on," Michael said

"She's in hospital."

"What!?!" I gasped.

"I'm so shocked." I went on.
"What do you mean she's in hospital?"

"She had an accident at precisely
one-fifty-seven this afternoon."

Michael seemed to lose his easy
attitude. He looked stern and almost
official. "What happened? How did it
happen?"

"She was hit by a lorry. A
delivery van. Someone saw her cross
against the light."

"Oh, *mon Dieu!*" I leaned back
against the desk. But Renee in
hospital was not good news,

"Why would she - " Michael
started and then checked himself.

"This is rather a shock."

"Why are you looking for me?" I
ventured.

"She had your name in her purse."

"My name? What do you. Mean?"

"I mean Mademoiselle, that she
had it written in her purse."

"Oh."

"Whatever for?"

"That is what I want to know,"
retorted the officer.

"Ok, then what questions do you
have for me?"

"Did you know Renee Beauvoir
well?"

"We've worked together here in
this room for over four years. That
is about it. She kept to herself. She
never spoke much about her personal

life. Neither of us shared this sort
of thing with each other."

"Do you know her next of kin?"

"No." I replied, with a shake of
my head. I could tell Ronan was
watching me.

"This is very difficult."

"Why don't you ask her boss?"
Ronan asked coolly. "I can take you
to his office, officer."

The officer looked rather
disturbed by this proposal. "Fine,
I'll go"

Michael took the officer away to
search for Crelon.

When it seemed that it was safe,
I decided to go to the cafeteria to
find something to drink. The release
of stress from that visitor was

palpable in my bones. I did not like
the way he looked at me. Why would
Renee have my name in her purse? And
why would she cross the street across
the light? These questions swirled in
my mind as I went into the lift.
There were others in the lift and it
seemed as though the news of Renee's
accident had spread for they were
conversing about her demise. Someone
looked at me and smiled slightly.

"You knew Renee Beauvoir, did you
not?" She asked.

"I worked in the same lab, but
not very well as a person."

'Renee was a loner, was she not?"

"She had her life," I shrugged
and then looked away to tell them I
preferred not to discuss anything

further.

Ronan came to find me as I was halfway through my coffee. He looked seriously at me. "I think we should visit Renee. Crelon is on his way there. Then," a smile touched his lips. "We can have our evening together."

We found the news that Renee had died of her injuries.

Michel met us with the news. "She's gone."

"That's too bad," Ronan said. "I think I'll take Agnes back to her home. She's had too much of all this."

Michel nodded. He looked at me and said, "I'll see you tomorrow, eh?"

I said nothing and Ronan pulled
me away towards the revolving doors of
the hospital.

Chapter Nineteen

When we arrived at the hospital, we found the news that Renee had died of her injuries.

Michel met us with the news. "She's gone."
"That's too bad," Ronan said. "I think I'll take Agnes back to her home. She's had too much of all this."

Michel nodded. He looked at me and said, "I'll see you tomorrow, eh?"

I said nothing and Ronan pulled me away towards the revolving doors of the hospital. We hailed a cab and while we sat together Ronan reached for my hand. "Your hand is cold. Don't worry, Agnes. This will pass."

"I can't feel good, Ronan. First it was Dorian, now It's Renee. What's happening?" I shook my head forlornly. "I'm tempted to quit working in that lab."

"Maybe you should."

I looked up at him, His face was inscrutable. "Maybe I should." I continued talking. "You know, with Renee gone and before her Dorian, there will be so much more for me to do to take up the slack."

"If you think that's wise, by all means, resign." He seemed to read her mind because he added, "Don't worry if you think you'll be letting him down, He has enough resources to hire more people.:

"I think you may be right," I replied,

He looked at his watch and said, "Its almost five in the afternoon, Why don't I drop you off and then I'll pick you after an hour so we can go for our dinner?:

I felt so much better after we had discussed my qualms. We said goodbye as he stood at my door with me. He made the cab driver wait until he was finished saying goodbye for a while,

Then, he leaned over and kissed me on
the lips. The contact was
electrifying. Not like when Paul
would kiss me. I felt like swooning
and I had to hold on to the doorknob
to keep from swaying,

Ronan smiled down at me and said,
"I;ll be back,"

I went into my apartment and found
it dark already. Sylvie was nowhere
to be found but when I walked into my
bedroom she was sitting on my bed, her
silky tail flicking as she watched me.
"Sylvie, how good you are," I said
and went to pet her.

I went back to the kitchen area and
put some of her cat food on a saucer
and placed it on the fireplace where
she would usually lounge. Sylvie
followed me and started to crouch over
her food and eat.

I decided to talk to Madame Cortes
and she was very nice when I told her
that I really wanted to work in her
cafe. "What day do you want to start,
Agnes?" She asked.

"I can start in a couple of days."

"Would this job be the right one for you, Agnes?" Her words told me she seemed to understand.

"I'll have to think of my future. I might take a course in the college and see whether I can work as a restaurateur and help you with you business."

"Ah, that's good. I want to be current with what is happening. I'm too busy to study these things. Your education will help me."

We agreed that I would start in two days. Then I went to the computer and wrote Michel Crelon an email saying that I was quitting as of today.

Chapter Twenty-One

Preparing for my real date with
Ronan was a thing that I would always
remember. I had a dress that I hardly
used but it was a classic thing that
appealed to me when I had gone
shopping some years ago. The dress
was a chiffon dress with a light
sprinkling of floral designs. I tried
it on and it still fit me. I wore a
pair of satin shoes that had a sling
back that I had bought from a
designer's store, which had already
gone out of business. It was a steal

when I purchased it. The other thing
I had was a small purse that I put
some of my essentials in like my keys
and a credit card and lipstick.

Ronan arrived and surveyed me.
The light in his eyes told me he
approved. "Shall go in my chariot,
Mademoiselle?" He asked with a smile.

"By all means."

We went to a posh restaurant and
he ordered a four course meal. Our
conversation was somewhat clumsy for
we couldn't seem to get away from the
subject of work. Then he said, "I
heard you resigned today."

"Yes I did."

"Why today?"

"I thought that it was best to
quit today. I had a conversation with
Madame Cortes who owns the restaurant
nearby. I think it would be relief
from working in a lab."

"That makes sense to me. You are
better for having quit. I will be
going back to Oxford in a few days
time."

That statement made my heart
sink. I lifted my eyes to his and
asked, "Is that so? I will be sorry
to see you go."

"You don't have to worry. I'll
back to visit."

"When will that be, Ronan?" I
fingered the wineglass and then
decided to drink the wine, to hide my
crestfallen heart.

"I will be returning to see to
what is going to happen to Crelon's
lab." He sounded mysterious. " I
have to confess that Crelon's lab is
going through hell."

"And why are you needing to watch
it go to hell?"

He said nothing at first. And

then he changed the subject by saying,
"I'll tell you when I'm allowed to."

The rest of the evening we had a
private conversation about us. "Tell
me why you haven't been married before
now?" Ronan asked.

"I never found anyone else, until
- " I bit my lip. Should I tell him
he was the one that I fell for?

"Until when?" He sounded
interested, but he kept on with his
meal, savoring the food and looking
quite confident as he did so.

"Until you." I decided to do the
thing to tell him he mattered to me.

"You were always there when I was in a
fix, at the lab. And we had a good
time going to take meals in the
restaurants. I always felt so much
better in the lab knowing you were
there if I needed you." When I said
all these I felt suddenly vulnerable.
I had bared my heart to this man who
hadn't said much in the sense of
loving me. But his next words were
able to lift up my sagging spirits.

"I also feel something special
for you, Agnes. I have fallen in love
with you," said Ronan.

He reached for my hand across the
table and held it in his. His hand
felt so secure and I returned his

grasp.

"Then what about us?   You are
leaving."

"No not leaving. I'm going to
return and I'll see about finding a
place to work here in Paris," he
said.

I smiled at him widely and my
heart danced a small jig. I was a
happy woman, a happy girl, really. As
though her best friend had come to say
those words, and that there would be
life with him soon.

"I think we should finish our
supper and continue this conversation

at your place, alright?" Ronan asked.

We did as he said, and I was aloft in my own thoughts about how he felt for me. I was so happy.

We rode back home to my place in each other's arms. The cab driver turned a deaf ear and a blind eye to what went on in the back seat. Ronan kissed me and murmured in my ear, those sweet words of love and it made me melt into his arms.

When we arrived, we ignored Sylvie and went straight to my room. We were enveloped with a romance that far surpassed what I had with Paul.

Ronan undressed me slowly on the bed as he leaned over and kissed me on the mouth, our tongues swaying against each other. I was half naked and he had taken his shirt off and I marveled at his muscular frame. Soon we were naked and he was all over me and I felt a shiver of delight when finally he entered me. I put my fist in my mouth when he made me come for fear that I would be shouting with ecstasy. Ronan made love to me again and in his quiet way made me forget all about anything or anyone.

We lay in bed afterwards in an afterglow and he held me in his arms and made me feel so cherished. It was a magical night for us. Ronan said he

loved me over and over again and I
told him that I loved him more than
anyone.

He looked down at me with a
questioning look. "Better than anyone
else, Agnes, my love?"

"Infinitely better, my dear
Ronan,"

Chapter Twenty-Two

My last day at Crelon's lab
started out indifferently. I went to
see him to confirm that he received my
email. Oddly enough, he didn't try to
dissuade me. He merely grunted and
said, "You can pack up your stuff,
leave your notebooks behind and I'll
get someone else to do your job."

I left his office feeling better

and went off to do as he said. The
absence of Renee was freeing as well.
There was nobody who would be looking
over my shoulder like she did.

The door opened and Ronan
entered. He gave me a special smile
that made me remember what happened
the night before. "Ahem," said Ronan,
"What are we up to today?"

"I'm packing my personal things.
I've spoken to Michel about leaving
and he's indifferent."

"That's fine. Do you need me to
help you?"

"No, I only have some of my

personal stuff. It won't take long."

"Will I see you tonight?" Then he slapped his head and said, "I'll be busy tonight. I'll call you instead and ask how your day went is that good?"

I stifled a sense of feeling disappointed that he wasn't going to see me tonight. "I'll wait for your call."

That moment there was a sound of excitement outside the door. "What's happening?" I asked him.

"I think there's a few things that are happening."

He sounded mysterious.

We went outside and the police were everywhere. "Where is Dr Crelon's office, *M'sieur*?" Asked one of the officers. He held a document in his hand.

"Just around the corner. You can't miss it." Ronan told me afterwards to go back to my lab and start packing.

The police had disappeared by the time that I left the laboratory. I went home with a small box of my things and contemplated the idea of becoming someone in the restaurant

business. It was a huge idea, and it
made me feel somewhat anxious. I
wasn't anyone who wanted to run a
restaurant. I merely wanted to be
part of the staff.

I went home and made supper and
served Sylvie her meal. I decided to
put on the news and catch what was
happening in the world. The television
flared into view and there was news of
trouble in a laboratory that was on
Crelon's building. I froze. Was this
the cause of the visit from the
police? I thought to myself. I saw
the news more intently. There was a
scene where they were leading Michel
Crelon away from the building. He was
escorted by the police. The

newsreader said he was suspected of
dealing cocaine from his laboratory.

I felt stricken with fear. Why
did I not know? Perhaps it was best
he kept it a secret from anyone else.
Who were the people in the lab who
helped him with this disgusting crime?

I shut the TV off and went back
to eat my meal. Then the phone rang.
It was Ronan. "Did you see the news?"
I asked him before he could say
anything.

"Oh, the Crelon arrest?" He
answered, "Yes, I was there when they
arrested him."

"How did it happen?"

"I'll tell you later," he
replied. "Look, I'll come by tomorrow
and visit the restaurant you work in,
would that work for you?"

"Yes I'd love to see you there,"
I replied, joyfully, all thought of
Michel's arrest had flown from my
mind. The sound of Ronan's voice made
it happen. "I love you Ronan."

"And I love you," and with that
he rang off.

Chapter Twenty-Four

The days without Ronan were spent
at Madame Cortes' restaurant, learning
the recipes and procedures in checking
out patrons. I served breakfast and
lunch and had a forty-five minute
break where I sat in one of the tables
eating my afternoon snack.

I heard little more about
Crelon's problems there and the
newspapers had a very brief story
about his arrest. I did not know more

about it until on the third day of
working at the Cortes' restaurant, I
received a call from Ronan who was in
town from Oxford. He said, "What
about if we met for a late afternoon
meal at your restaurant?"

"That would be fine," I replied
and we rang off.

That afternoon, he appeared
looking unlike his usual appearance.
Gone were his casual jacket and slacks
and he wore a suit and had his hair
groomed.

We kissed lingeringly amidst all
of the patrons in the restaurant and
they all looked interestedly and then
ignored us as we sat down to order a

meal for each other.

"What's new, then, Ronan?" I
asked.

"I'm here to tell you that the
Crelon lab was a fake, like I said. He
used people like you to do regular
work but he hired criminals like
Dorian and Renee to carry out his
cocaine purifying process."

"Cocaine purifying?" I echoed,
surprise in my voice. "He was doing
this under our noses?"

"Yes."

"And he used Dorian and Renee?"

"Yes."

"And you knew?" I asked him,
thinking he was really coming out with
the truth about himself.

"I knew because I observed

everything and found out about it."
Ronan looked at me seriously. "I work
for the Interpol, Agnes. This is my
work. I spy on these scientific
places but I don't always go in to
arrest them. I merely give the
information to my superiors."

I leaned back and gazed at him
with surprise and a mingling pride.

"Oh, my God, you are amazing!" I
exclaimed.

He prodded me. "Go and eat your
food. I have to stay over with you
tonight."

"I'm sure I'll be happy tonight,
Ronan."

"You were lucky they didn't get
you to do their work."

"But I worked on the biological

stuff, nothing to do with chemistry. That purifying of cocaine is something that I have no mind about."

"That's true. Dorian did it and Renee and Dorian sold it to the addicts. Crelon was also dealing it with high stakes drug dealers and used his travel time to do it all over Europe."

"How very amazing."

"Isn't it though? I suggest very strenuously that you never work for a laboratory again, Agnes."

"Don't worry, Ronan. The work I do here is very good and it helps to feed people. The neighbourhood is good and we have good meals to serve them."

He reached into his pocket and

gave me a small box that was black satin covered. "Here is my wish, Agnes. Will you marry me?"

I gazed in awe at the box. I opened it. Inside was a ring that had a solitaire diamond in the center. I almost swooned. "Ohh, Ronan!"

"Will you?"

"Oh, yes, I'll marry you!"